12 OXEN

UNDER

THE SEA

STORIES

CRAIG

BERNARDINI

newamericanpress
✳
Milwaukee, Wisconsin

newamericanpress
✳
Milwaukee, Wisconsin

12 Oxen Under the Sea
© 2025 BY CRAIG BERNARDINI

Printed in the United States of America
ISBN 978-1-941561-34-8

Cover + Book Design by Angelo Maneage
Author Photograph by Sean Graff

For ordering information, please contact:
INGRAM BOOK GROUP
ONE INGRAM BLVD.
LA VERGNE, TN 37086
(800) 937-8000
ORDERS@INGRAMBOOK.COM

For media and event inquiries, please visit:
WWW.NEWAMERICANPRESS.COM

PROUD MEMBER

"The volatile fictions in Craig Bernardini's collection reveal an electric imagination shot through with fever-dream logic and a comic skew serious as death. *12 Oxen Under the Sea* is eccentric in the very best sense of the word."

LANCE OLSEN, AUTHOR OF *ABSOLUTE AWAY*

"Craig Bernardini's *12 Oxen Under the Sea* eviscerates the soft, white underbelly of middle-class fiction. Babies catch fire and burn tableside, fathers transform into swamp things, and a pair of neighborhood freaks share names with an only child. What else to do but cast every last scrap of our identities into deep waters, and when nothing else remains, ourselves? Inhabited by assassin pianists, futureless boys whacking Ramen noodle hockey pucks across thin ice, whale displays hiding bones of fetid children who've crawled into their sanctuary, and rooms where things just won't stay still, this prize-winning debut will knock your socks off, and a whole lot more."

MICHAEL GILLS, AUTHOR OF *BURNING DOWN MY FATHER'S HOUSE*

"What a wonder this book of stories is! In the absurdist, fantastic tradition of Kafka, Barthelme and Steven Millhauser, Craig Bernardini's debut collection is very dark and very funny. Plus, every one of these 12 stories has a river of heartbreak running through, a poignant reflection on the raging chaos of our 21st century world. An interminable hotel fire, a museum in whose crevices a kid may sequester himself, and a mysterious depthless pond are just some of the artifacts that Bernardini plunders for metaphorical, indeed poetic, treasures. Bravo!"

KAREN BRENNAN, AUTHOR OF *RABBIT IN THE MOON: THE MEXICO STORIES*

for Tanya

CONTENTS

12 OXEN

UNDER

THE SEA

And he made a molten sea, ten cubits from the one brim to the other:
it was round all about, and his height was five cubits: and a line of thirty
cubits did compass it round about.

It stood upon twelve oxen, three looking toward the north, and three
looking toward the west, and three looking toward the south, and three
looking toward the east: and the sea was set above upon them, and all
their hinder parts were inward.

1 KINGS 7.23, 25

FAT KID

FAT KID: A CHUBBY TWENTYSOMETHING FROM YONKERS WITH A MOP of reddish-brown hair. Fond of wearing seal-gray chamois shirts over band T's. Photographed one night at an Inveterate Villifier show, at Brooklyn's Club Dump. Orff, Villifier's frontman, growls at the left edge of the frame, hair slicked to his shoulders, right arm a sleeve of mail, mic doublefisted. He is half-turned from the lens, which points crowdward, at Fat Kid and his ilk. Fat Kid: his right fist raised before him in arm-wrestling position, mouth wide, cheeks flushed, eyes button-black. He is incandescent with rage. He is in The Zone.

We started seeing that picture whenever we opened our emails or got a text. In a matter of days it had become our avatar of choice. It surfaced in random YouTube vids, Fat Kid, but cropped from his original surroundings, like an icon for our veneration. He mutated as he grew, went grayscale, chiaroscuro, Warhol; he countered familiarity with abstraction, Cubism, stick-figure, synecdoche (a clenched fist, an open mouth). And then one day the original photo, Orff and all, popped up on the tickers of the big internet newsfeeds: Fat Kid was now a bona fide phenomenon, if not yet a proper name. Yahoo earned the distinction of the first easily-traceable use of the words *fat kid* (in "Fan's Musical Rage Goes Viral"), which appeared once, uncapitalized, and inside of a quotation. The source went unnamed; it could have been any of us. A Facebook page was born, where our newly-christened Fat Kid could be poked at will, and left cryptic messages. If we image-googled Fat Kid, we were faced with a wall of thumbnails, like windows in a virtual highrise where Fat Kid was the only tenant. It was pages and pages before any other fat kids appeared.

Soon Fat Kid grew bigger than the net, as websites all claiming to be the official Fat Kid store started hawking T-shirts, posters, key chains, wallets, lighters, mugs, stickers, you name it. There was a table at every show covered with Fat Kid merchandise, and it became all the rage to come wearing a Fat Kid shirt, no matter who was on the bill, because Fat Kid was *always* on the bill. There were so many variations on the Fat Kid design that you never went to a show without spotting a cutting-edge Fat Kid on some preening fellow fan; and there was no better way to one-up the guy next to you than to show up in a Fat Kid shirt more obscure than his. Bands even started to feel the pinch at their own merch tables, or at least they felt threatened enough to circulate a petition, where fans would pledge not to consume any more Fat Kid products. The petition was called Fuck Fat Kid.

It never got any traction. But who was counting? *We* didn't need Fat Kid products to feel Fat Kid. We started saying things like, Fuck, I went totally Fat Kid at that God Forbid show last night, or, Holy shit, I saw you up there—you were mad Fat Kid! We would get texts at shows expressing the hope that it was Fat Kid, and we would respond with the initials F.K., followed by several exclamation marks, to communicate that it was, indeed, Fat Kid. Buzz around some new something-or-other? #fatkid went bananas. Songs were Fat Kid, albums were ranked on a scale of 1 to Fat Kid, bands were either Fat Kid or not-Fat Kid, and sometimes went from one to the other. If you nudged your friend at a show and shouted "Fat Kid," it meant you were about to freak the fuck out. Because Fat Kid couldn't sell out, he couldn't break up, he couldn't grow old, he wouldn't go gently, and he absolutely would never ever die. The music, the ambience, the sound, the whole *scene* was Fat Kid. He was our ideal child, the spirit of metal incarnate, made the hulking, epic flesh we always knew it to be.

Fat Kid's friends told him he needed to get a hold of himself, that he should copyright and merchandise himself, shit, he should be making millions, instead of letting a bunch of assholes he didn't even know many money off of him. This made sense to Fat Kid, but the more he thought about it, the more a muddle it seemed. After all, he was only Fat Kid *because* of the picture, he had never been Fat Kid *until* the picture, so what more claim did he have to Fat Kid than anybody else?

He too started wearing a Fat Kid shirt to shows. Maybe he thought he could hide behind it, but we all recognized him, we would say, Hey, it's Fat Kid, we would take pictures of ourselves with him, make him make the face, strike the pose. Fat Kid would quip that he was going to rent a booth and charge a nickel a shot. He never did.

It wasn't long before he was walking around telling everybody he wasn't really Fat Kid, he just looked like him. And who could blame him? There were precious few perks to being Fat Kid, this though we all claimed to envy and admire and even worship him, to want to be him. It's not like he ever got laid for being Fat Kid. Hell, he never even got kissed for being Fat Kid. The most he ever got to do was slip his arms around a couple of girls' waists; they would purse their lips a hair from either cheek, so close they grazed the skin, and their warm breath tickled him when they told their boyfriends to hurry up—and then the flash would go off, and it would be over, just like that.

He stopped denying he was Fat Kid, and instead started to claim that he was more than Fat Kid. But who wants to hear from Fat Kid that he's more than Fat Kid? Who wants to make it a philosophical discussion? Fine, Fat Kid thought, and started to ignore everyone who asked him to be Fat Kid. We started calling him Hey. Asshole instead. Yet, on the rare occasions that he did stop, and that he decided to humor us, he could no longer muster the energy to be Fat Kid. We would say, Wait a minute, you're not Fat Kid after all, or, Are you sure you're Fat Kid? or, Man, that is the weakest Fat Kid I ever saw. He recognized our disappointment—kids at a fair who find the rides are all closed—but what could he do to assuage us? Better to silently admit he was an impostor, and move on.

He remembered wanting us to think he wasn't Fat Kid. Now he had his wish. But how could he convince us he was more than Fat Kid when we didn't think he was Fat Kid to begin with?

One day somebody said to him, You know, it's fine you're not Fat Kid, but you don't have to bag on Fat Kid while you're at it. It occurred to him that only Fat Kid could kill Fat Kid. He decided then and there to ham being Fat Kid in front of Fat-Kid enthusiasts. He would give us Fat Kid until we choked. He would make us believe he was Fat Kid and murder Fat Kid in one stroke. As soon as he thought he'd been recognized, he would rush up and shout, Hey, look at me, I'm Fat Kid, and lampoon the pose, up-yoursing with the fist, and contorting his face into a simpering travesty of the original. Sometimes we snapped pictures of him anyway. All the better, Fat Kid thought. Let it proliferate, let it multiply like the seeds of the patriarchs. He even started to vandalize Fat Kid merchandise: all varieties of mustaches on the face, graffiti penises ballooning from the fist, or prodding into the open mouth. He felt guilty, but he was a man on a mission, a suicide pact with the scene.

As it turned out, there was no such thing as too much Fat Kid. The words "too much" and "fat kid" simply did not belong in the same oration. Nor could he combat with mere images what had already blossomed into an idea. And so the cult of Fat Kid grew.

Fat Kid lost weight. He cut his hair, grew a real mustache, and started wearing glasses. We still recognized him, or at least we thought we did. We would ask that question, a meaningless, convictionless question, cautiously approached: Are you Fat Kid? To which he might nod wearily, or pretend not to understand.

The truth was he had begun to doubt he was Fat Kid. It had been somebody else in that picture; he had just taught himself a convincing impersonation, and then gone around making like a false prophet. He kept going to shows; he told himself that there he would find the real Fat Kid, or maybe prove to himself that he was Fat Kid after all. Instead, he found himself staring around at the crowd, our phones all held up. Flash, flash, flash … who would be immolated next? He ducked, he cringed. It was like dodging bullets in a blind alley. Ridiculous, for what could we do to him that we hadn't done already? He lost more weight; he lost more weight, his skin turned gray, sagged like old sail from a shipwreck of bone. Too tired to stand, he stayed at the bar, never even bothering to swivel around and face the stage. He only watched himself, if there was a mirror behind the bottles, trying not to move a muscle.

And he asked his image, silently, a sneer in his voice: Are you Fat Kid?

Said the image: You're a monkey's uncle.

One night he happened to let slip to the stranger beside him that he was Fat Kid. He heard himself say it, and, clearing his throat, he said it again, a little more loudly. He even did the best he could, yes, the very best he could, tired, tipsy, and without standing: the pose; the face. Held it: one, two, three, four, five. The stranger, regarding him over one shoulder, said, Wow. I guess you are Fat Kid. But the position of his body, and the tone of his voice, convinced Fat Kid that he was being patronized. He opened the fist into a dismissive wave and turned back to his drink.

I just imagined you …

Fatter?

Bigger, the man corrected.

I lost weight, Fat Kid said.

Clearly.

They faced each other at the bar.

The thing is? Even when I was Fat Kid? I never felt … that … fat.

Oh, but I did.

Yeah?

Sure. Everybody did.

Everybody but me, Fat Kid pouted. And then: How did it feel?

When I was Fat Kid? When I was Fat Kid, the man said, in the voice of someone recalling a youthful love, a battle where a brother had perished. Deep breath through the nose. I felt … like I weighed eight hundred pounds. No: a ton. Not that English shit, either. I'm talking metric.

Like that dude they buried in a piano case.

In the *Guinness Book of World Records*?

Yeah. Remember him?

Dude was my hero.

Mine too. We used to hide that book in our desks at school.

The dude with the fingernails always creeped me out …

Fat Kid sighed. Like they needed a crane to move you. Right?

Two. But they always snapped. Like masts in a hurricane.

The Grand Canyon must have looked like a crack in the sidewalk. There's nothing grand about it, my friend.

The crater left by the K-T meteor must have looked like … like pockets on a billiards table.

The Pacific basin was my duck pond.

The world was too small for you, Fat Kid whispered.

Some claim to have seen Fat Kid since, slinking around the murkiest corners of our favorite clubs on particularly brutal nights. A figure so pale he approaches transparency, a spar of his former self, receding even were he to stand still, halving himself without ever quite perishing, dissolving into the dank, hot air like a sugar-cube. If someone thinks they have spotted him, a cry goes up from the crow's-nest of the balcony; we look up to see a pointing finger, we all turn its direction with our phones cocked. A cannonade of flashes. It could be a rumor, a mistake, a ruse. The pictures have all been uploaded, you can judge for yourself. Like pictures of Nessie, or Bigfoot. Like any other community we have our believers. But then there are those of us who say there never was a Fat Kid, that the whole thing was a fable from the start, a collectively-scripted fiction. Through it, we affirmed and continue to affirm ourselves; and perhaps this makes believers of all of us, after a fashion.

THE DEATH
OF THE PIANIST

HIS ASSASSINATION

THE LIGHTS DIMMED, THE STAGE DOOR WAS CRACKED AND THEN swung wide, the pianist shuffled out, bent slightly forward, arms pumping. He was the sinker on a plumb-line drawn by the gravity of applause. As if its patter were the audible expression of that force, like the crackling of an electrical wire.

He offered a series of furtive bows, each little more than a nod, to different sections of the audience. He was stiff as a bird, and nearly as devoid of expression. No fiddling with the height or distance of the piano bench, no tossing of his coattails; the heroic opening chords of the "Hammerklavier" rang out in the auditorium before the applause had a chance to die down.

I wanted to remark to the woman sitting next to me that the pianist was identical to my uncle, who in turn resembled my grandfather more than my father did, who resembled me. But her gaze was already fixed through her opera-glasses. Beside her, her husband appeared to sleep.

Less than a minute later the stage door opened again, and a second pianist appeared, walking with the same stoop-shouldered gait as the first, and looking just as much like my uncle.

This pianist made a bee-line for the piano.

Excluding his dress, manner of walking, and resemblance to my uncle, I had no evidence as yet that the second figure was a pianist. He might have been a tenor. It would of course have been highly irregular for a soloist to appear unannounced at this stage in the performance. It occurred to me, too, that the "Hammerklavier," as the name indicates, is a sonata for unaccompanied pianoforte. But perhaps it was a surprise, a celebration. A birthday.

The second pianist stopped a few feet behind the first, drew a pistol from his tuxedo jacket, and fired two shots in rapid succession into the first pianist's back.

The first pianist played until the instant the first bullet struck. Then he raised both hands high above the keyboard in the sort of gesture one expects to fill a caesura. With the second bullet his face contorted, as if he had forgotten to emote, and he collapsed forward onto the keyboard.

Together with the echo of the shots, that final, profoundly mysterious chord resonated through the auditorium, until the assassin of the first pianist took the corpse by one wrist and, with a brief glissando, tugged it over the far edge of the bench.

The corpse lay with its back to us while the assassin of the first pianist returned the pistol to his jacket pocket and stood facing the crowd between the bench and the keyboard, one hand resting on the instrument. Even from the balcony I could see the holes in the tuxedo jacket.

The second pianist delivered a series of crisp bows before sitting. There was a smattering of applause, and some coughing and rustling, and a loud shush from an offended patron. For the second pianist had, like the first, begun playing before the noise had settled: the "Hammerklavier" again, from precisely the point where the first pianist had left off.

My ears were still ringing from the shots, and I remarked mentally how startling was the sound of a pistol fired in a place built to catch the faintest whisper. But as the ringing faded so did my memory of the event, and with the exception of the body on the stage it was soon possible to believe that the sonata had never been interrupted.

Some minutes later the second pianist finished the first movement and, with hardly a breath, plunged into the jaunty scherzo. I could hear him humming in a light monotone under his breath.

A third pianist appeared, with an identical shuffling gait to the first two, and looking just as much like my uncle. He moved with the same steadfastness of purpose as the second.

This time, an older gentleman in the first few rows stood and shouted something at the second pianist, but he was roundly booed and shushed by other audience members in his vicinity, and by one in mine, and with a wave of his hand he retook his seat.

The second pianist was too immersed in the intricacies of the scherzo to notice either the audience member or the third pianist, the second assassin. I braced for the shot, though I refused to plug my ears.

The third pianist dispatched the second with a single shot to the back of the head.

On receiving the bullet, the second pianist pitched forward, his head ricocheted off the instrument, and as he was flung backwards his knees caught on the underside of the keyboard, so that, a moment later, his body hung suspended across the bench, back arched, arms thrown back, head nearly touching the stage, like a backstroker trapped in mid-start.

The piano had never looked so much like an instrument of torture.

From the stage door there emerged two new players: an usher in a bright red tux, and a lank, white-haired man in regular business attire.

The usher, who was bulky and a head taller than either of the other two, occupied himself with the bodies while the third pianist smoked—he had exchanged his pistol for a cigarette case immediately after the murder. The other man, whom I imagined to be an undertaker, looked on.

Because the bullet had refracted off the second pianist's skull into the soundboard, or because pieces of the skull had been ejected into the cabling, or because of the force with which the shattered remains of the second pianist's head had been catapulted into the keyboard— whatever the reason, or for all three, the piano hummed uncannily, as if the ghost of the second pianist refused to remove its fingers from the keys, daring us to applaud before the last trace of sound had faded.

But applaud we did, a slow, hard, steady applause, a sound I associate with house-framing. Tentative at first, localized, it was by degrees picked up by other members of the audience, until this laborious applause thundered from every corner of the auditorium.

The third pianist bowed quickly and stiffly, with that familiarly inscrutable, sparrow-like expression on his face.

Meanwhile the usher removed the second pianist's body. He took it by both wrists and tugged until the hips slid off the bench, and with a flutter of coattails the corpse slumped concave. One black shoe caught briefly under the keyboard, until the usher whipped the body like a bedsheet, dislodging the shoe from both the instrument and the foot. The corpse was then dragged stage left, picking up momentum as it went, leaving a glistening streak behind it.

That immaculate, abandoned shoe lay on its side next to the sostenuto pedal.

Watching the second pianist's single stocking foot quavering as the body to which it belonged was removed saddened me.

But the shoe! The shoe embodied all the tragedy of great Romantic art.

The usher soon returned for the second body, which he hoisted over his shoulder and fireman-carried stage left. As the arms swung behind him, trickles of blood ran out of the cuffs and the collar, off the tips of the fingers and the nose and earlobes, leaving a discreet, irregular pattern.

The woman beside me followed this action assiduously through her opera-glasses. Her husband, awake now, consulted his program.

I could swear I had seen the usher, while he was bent like Atlas before the body, remove something from the first pianist's coat and slip it into his own pocket. But at the moment I reached out to tug at the woman's sleeve, she wet her lips with her tongue, and my hand sprang back into my lap.

A few people applauded the usher, who nodded before disappearing again through the stage door.

The second man, the one I had presumed to be an undertaker, turned out to be a piano tuner, and he went about his work while the third pianist smoked. He tuned with such seeming gravity and near-mechanical concentration, almost with an air of fatalism, that I kept expecting him to turn to the third pianist and shake his head, as if to say, *This patient is lost.*

The lights came up, a few people stood and stretched, though the intermission (such as it was) had lasted less than a minute before a bell informed us that it was time to resume our seats.

The tuner frowned at the bell and packed up his tools, and a moment later his gaunt frame was swallowed by the light of the stage door. Almost immediately the third pianist extinguished his cigarette under his heel and took his place at the bench. He removed a handkerchief from the same pocket he had the cigarettes and the pistol earlier, opened it with the practiced authority of a magician, and ran it once up and down the keys, smearing blood along the ivory. The action seemed more ritual than practical, particularly when he dabbed his forehead, leaving a smudge of blood there. His hands alighted on the keyboard. I braced for the shot.

Because he never got to play a single note, I am unsure whether to refer to him as a pianist, or simply as the assassin of the second pianist. Yet, in all other respects and particulars, he resembled the first two: the bowed, stoop-shouldered half-plummet of a parachutist through the stage door; the combined intensity and aloofness of his manner; the total absence of hesitation when he stopped, drew, and fired into the back of the second pianist's head. And now the poise, the singular poise with which he rested his hands on the keyboard, the instant before meeting his death. I did not need to hear him play a note; of all of them, he was the truest musician.

In fact, I am convinced that he never intended for his fingers to strike the keys, just as I am convinced that the second and first pianists were also aware of the evening's program: that they lived, so to speak, in the shadow of the gun—as do we all, though they with infinitely greater consciousness of this fact—in the trajectory of a bullet fired at the moment of our conception, approaching unerringly but ever so slowly, or perhaps only from an unfathomably great distance, and whose whine we can hear in the silence of an auditorium when we incline our ear musicward. This and this alone explains the majesty of their collective performance, as if each and all were involved in raising a cathedral. Who knows but that the first pianist only practiced the first twenty bars of the "Hammerklavier"; and yet, he took the bullet as if he were convinced he would play the entire sonata, and play it again and again in concerts for years to come. How else to explain the aplomb with which the second pianist assumed the first's labor, and the equally catastrophic ease with which he accepted his demise? Who knows how long they had spent rehearsing their deaths in and through that monumental sonata?

As if he had had a sudden change of heart, the third pianist, assassin of the second, drew his hands away from the keyboard and rested them palm-up in his lap. The woman gripped her glasses yet more tightly; her husband flipped madly through his program; the shot still rang in my ears. Then the third pianist keeled left, crumpling as he rocked sideways, until his shoulder came to rest on the bench. His head lolled like a doll's into empty space; his hands fell forward, so that one came to rest palm-down on his belly.

In that moment, he was no longer a pianist, but *a flower withering in a rain of lover's tears.*

I was shocked by the violence of the response. It wasn't just the applause, which erupted suddenly and simultaneously from all sides of the auditorium. The audience shouted and whistled and stamped their feet. And before I knew what was happening, several members of the first few rows, including two frail-looking women in evening gowns, had clambered up onto the stage to lay bouquets. I thought I recognized the man who had shouted at the second pianist among them, but lost him as more and more members of the audience stormed the stage. Soon the piano looked like a catafalque, and the crowd was sufficient to raise the body of the third pianist and pass it into the orchestra, where it traveled on a manicured sea up the left side of the hall and disappeared under the balcony overhang. The crowd seethed in its direction, trailing the body into the hot New

York night, whose sirens and engine-brakes now penetrated the auditorium through flung-open doors and windows.

The woman beside me lowered her glasses; I half-expected to see black rings around her eyes. She had started to tell me that it wasn't just the gesture, but the usher, the tuner, the brief raising of the house lights, the expectation of the music forever deferred, that made the final performance so clearly the pinnacle of the evening's program. But then she must have noticed the still-smoking pistol in my right hand, the missing fingers on the other, the smell of cordite in her nostrils, the gleam in my eye, the way my voice cracked when I said, "*Gesundheit!*" even though she hadn't sneezed. And then I was on the stairs, running down and down their crooked spirals, past the exclamations of "*Mon dieu!*" into the lobby, and out into the carnival of traffic and steam. The performance had only just begun, and I still had one bullet left.

SCARECROW

PEOPLES PLAYHOUSE IS A SMALL, INDEPENDENT, SADLY RUN-DOWN cinema located in the northwest corner of Greenwich Village. Upstairs, the molded tin ceiling rains tin flakes and tin dust onto the seats, prompting you to brush the cushions off before sitting down, or to bring a newspaper, as you might to the park. The seats, both upstairs and down, date from Peoples' original incarnation as a vaudeville house in the early twenties—you sink into them, as into the mattress in some skid row fleabag—and the armrests are worn by a near-century of elbows to a texture resembling bone. Even the restrooms are original, dank as tombs, with urinals like enamel sarcophagi. The air conditioning, which you can hear chugging away on hot summer days, is an exercise in futility; it is not rare to see patrons enter the theater with damp towels thrown over their heads and shoulders, like faux Bedouins.

The renovations of the seventies, which partitioned the theater into a multiplex, only multiplied Peoples' ills. The wall dividing the two boxcar-shaped downstairs theaters, and the ceiling between these and the smaller third carved from the balcony, are so minimally soundproofed that you can sometimes hear, say, the gunshots and war-whoops of a John Ford Western playing in theater 2 while you are trying to follow, say, a Bergman movie in theater 1. The screens hang about where an olio curtain might have hung; and because of this, the area that was once a stage—or, in theater 3, the alcove where the battens would have been—seems to recede into some secret nowhere; the screens themselves could be scrims; and the images projected take on the aspect of a shadow-play produced by live figures miming the action behind them. In theaters 1 and 2, before the lights go down, you might even notice a trail of shoeprints on the dusty boards between the lip of the stage and the screen, as if figures could pass through it unimpeded, and the photoplay bulged with three-dimensional life.

Negligence and disrepair help account for the generally poor attendance, although it may be that the theater never had adequate capital to undertake a real renovation. The city, whether for reasons of parsimony or patronage, has declined to landmark it. Peoples is further handicapped by its location at the middle of a quiet residential block; the laundromat in the basement of an adjacent brownstone is the only other business. The marquee, if it can be called that, is almost flush with the façade, so that even pedestrians passing on the opposite side of the narrow street have to crane their necks to see the names of current features. Nor does Peoples advertise—again, whether for lack of funds, or a general disinterest on the part of the management, it is difficult to tell. An internet search turns up no official, stable web presence, and only a handful of comments, all negative, appear in a few web-based city guides. All of this has helped to keep the clientele local. In return, neighborhood residents—many of whom were born and raised in the buildings where they live—seem to tolerate the theater's presence like that of an elderly relative they visit occasionally out of a sense of filial duty.

I had been living in New York for more than a year already when I discovered Peoples—a somewhat surprising fact, given my interest in older cinema, particularly films of the silent era, and my penchant for visiting revival houses. I could wile away whole afternoons immersed in a world of dramatic gestures and intertitles; when I emerged, around twilight, the city never looked quite the same. But then Peoples didn't just play old movies; it was an old theater, and old theaters—old things in general—aren't always easy to spot. It takes a certain amount of training, and a certain force of will. A desire. Most people don't have these, so they see nothing. Or what they see is like a photograph in an album, framed and cut off from everything else. People tend to see all things past in this way, like they are tourists of another time. But I had a nose for ferreting out such old places; and New York, where past and present are so deeply intertwined, where the contemporary continuously rubs shoulders with the ancient, and where, no matter how many times a neighborhood is built over, one turn of the shovel, one scratch of a nail, might uncover a priceless fossil—New York was the place to find them.

I was following an old man around the Village the day it happened. I did this from time to time, believing that another's routine, particularly that of an elderly person, might reveal to me some angle of the City, some bit of shadow, some unnamed cross-street that I had never noticed before. On this I was following a man I was almost certain I recognized. Perhaps it was only in that nagging city way:

encountering thousands of strangers on a daily basis, you can't help but begin to find one every now and then who looks a little familiar.

I remember the ticket seller playing solitaire in the box office, the five in change unexpectedly thrust back through the mousehole, the poster for Murnau's *Sunrise* in the vestibule. *Coming Soon!* the placard promised. There were a few such posters in the corridor leading to the concession area—Bergman's *Persona*, Antonioni's *Blow-up*, Wilder's *Sunset Boulevard*—which was divided by a red velour chain, although I was the only human traffic. I remember the Peter Lorre lookalike at the concession stand, pacing between the popcorn bin and the butter dispenser, as though preparing munitions against impending hordes. I remember the usher's bowtie and stud earrings, and that he did not look me in the eye when he tore my ticket. I can't remember the title of the picture I went to see, or which theater it was in, though I'm certain it wasn't upstairs, and that it was a talkie. I'm also certain of the following: that it was a matinee; that it started late; and that there were several previews, all for films half a century old, with those lovely wipes and irises, snippets of dialogue that fell into black holes, and the high earnestness of the voiceover. I remember that there were perhaps twenty other people in the theater, not a one under sixty, and that they occasionally spoke to each other, as might be expected, in voices louder than a whisper. The sound system winced at loud noises, like a gun-shy animal, and there were three minutes of darkness while somebody wrestled to change a reel, and during which I listened to the patrons cough and the dialogue unspool in the next theater. Although I couldn't make out the words, it was clear from the gatling speed and minimal cadences that the movie was from the forties. At some point I shifted from one sore hip to the other and ran my palms up and down the bone-smooth armrests; and I knew that, in some deep sense, I had arrived: the City, here, home. I was precisely where I wanted to be.

I went to Peoples twice, sometimes three times a week, usually on weekdays, always to a matinee. I had my customary seat in each theater; there were never enough people in the audience to fear my seats would be taken. I even started to imagine they bore plaques with my name on them, in imitation of the more upscale revival houses. I must have seen a hundred pictures there in a year, many more than once. Silents, foreign films, musicals, newsreels, shorts. The picture didn't matter; *being there* mattered. It should therefore come as no surprise that the title of the film I was supposed to see on the day of the incident I am about to relate escapes me, just as does the title of the film I saw on the day I stumbled upon Peoples. I only remember that it happened in theater 2, and that the film was scheduled to begin at two-forty-five. I remember hoisting up my watch like an aquarium thermometer—five to three—winding it a few times, and dropping it back into my pocket.

As I sat waiting for the show to begin, staring at the coral-pink haze of the screen—unlike some other revival houses, Peoples never scrolled through ads prior to their screenings—I noticed music playing, very softly—so softly that, in the quieter moments, it fell entirely out of my hearing. Funny I hadn't noticed it before. I stopped chewing my popcorn and focused my full attention on the music, waiting for the next swell … there. The great, pensive strokes of an agonized *cantabile*. It was Rachmaninoff's second piano concerto. And no wonder I should recognize it. I had had a fairly serious love affair with Rachmaninoff in my teens. I even whistled along for a few bars, until all I could hear was my own whistling.

Even with the volume so low, the music had a way of sucking me in. Maybe it was the emotional memories the concerto prompted. Or maybe it was because of the volume: having it just on the edge of my consciousness in that way, having to focus all my attention and even hold my breath just to hear it. Somehow, this flirting with silence only multiplied the concerto's power, which lay, I decided, in the feeling of yearning it projected—a yearning which I myself now projected onto it, in my desire to hear.

As I have already indicated, lateness was not untypical for Peoples. Among other things, it meant that, no matter how slowly I ate, I tended to finish my popcorn before the movie had started. But I sensed there was a different reason this day: a matter of respect on somebody's part, perhaps the manager, perhaps the projectionist, not for the twenty-odd patrons gathered in theater 2, but for the integrity of the music. Whoever he was, he was loath to interrupt the movement, and perhaps the concerto as a whole.

So I patiently waited out the end of the first movement, alternately seduced and piqued; and sure enough, after a few seconds of silence during which no one moved a muscle, and even I held my breath in inexplicable anticipation, the second movement struck up—a little louder, despite its being the *Adagio*, than the first.

Now I couldn't help but feel a little cheated. I had bought my ticket in good faith, as I did every week, twice a week. I even became a bit demonstrative in my frustration, clucking my tongue and murmuring aloud, expecting, perhaps, that it would resonate with my fellow patrons—that they, too, would begin to exhibit signs of irritation, or confusion. And yet, I found that I could not justify my feelings to myself. I had no other plans, nothing more pressing to attend to. What's more, I had made a habit of buying my tickets sight-unseen. Could I think of anything more pleasant, really, than loitering away the afternoon listening along with two dozen other people to the quiet magnificence of a Rachmaninoff piano concerto?

Perhaps, I thought now, the projectionist—for some reason I had decided that he was the responsible party—was listening to the concerto in his booth, and we were just hearing its muffled echo. Or perhaps he was furiously trying to untangle the reel, and hoped that a little light music would stop the rankled patrons from mutiny. I looked behind me, up at the small square window, but with the house lights still up it was impossible to tell if anyone was there.

As for my fellow patrons: they hardly seemed like a group poised to revolt. In fact, they might all have been mannequins; I had to restrain myself from bending back and jostling the nearest one by the shoulder. A strange conviction stopped me: that I could not reach him. I could only *pretend* to touch him, by closing one eye.

At some point during the second movement I found that I could no longer contain my anxiety. Though I rose with the purpose of going to the lobby, I went up to the screen instead, or as near to the screen as the stage would permit. Approaching, I had the sense that the stage was not a chest-high riser with which I would collide, but the edge of a precipice over which I would tumble, into a coral-pink mist far below. Reaching out was reaching in; my hand grasped nothing, and the music only seemed soft because it emanated from a vast distance, as though it were the echo of music heard across a valley. Turning, I scanned the faces of my fellow patrons. A few had their heads bowed reverentially, but the majority stared straight ahead, their gazes fixed upon the screen behind me. They looked like the well-drugged residents of a rest home, or the members of some New Age cult greeting the arrival of the Mothership. On closer inspection, however, I noticed that their eyes tracked left and right, as though they were following some activity. I glanced behind me, wondering if perhaps the film had started—some silent image awaiting sound, or without a recorded soundtrack. But there was only that pink haze, undulating to the whisper of Rachmaninoff. Walking back up the aisle, I stopped beside each of the patrons sitting at the ends of their rows, leaning close enough to smell their perfumes and colognes, talc and tobacco, dental adhesives, urine. No matter how close I leaned, they did not appear to notice me. Even waving my hand before their eyes could not deflect their vision.

The usher who had ripped my ticket—the same one who always ripped my ticket—was not at his podium. The concessions area was dark. It was possible the stand had closed when the movie started. But the movie hadn't started. It was possible the concessions operator and the projectionist were one and the same person, and he closed the stand as soon as the line for the matinee screening had dissipated. It would explain why the movies always started a little late, and perhaps why there were occasionally a few minutes of murmuring darkness and exodus to the restrooms between reels.

The corridor leading to the vestibule was also empty and dark, although the light admitted by the glass doors at the far end was sufficient to navigate by. At the box office, the blinds were drawn, and no one answered when I rapped. Maybe the ticket-seller, not the concessions operator, was the projectionist. Or maybe ticket-seller, concessions operator and usher all sat up in the booth together, one unspooling lengths of film, the second measuring them, the third cutting them with a razor. When they held the frames up to the light, I saw a succession of images of myself, trapped in those little puncture-bordered squares, each one divided from the next by a hair's-breadth of time.

On the board above the box-office window three titles were listed, none of which I recognized. This much was fine; as I have indicated, I often bought my tickets sight-unseen.

It was just that all the showtimes were for evening.

Steadying myself against the window, I rapped again, waited, rapped harder, with my knuckles, with my fist. I was sure that little man was hiding inside, playing his endless game of solitaire.

My watch. It still said five minutes to three. I put it away without bothering to wind it again.

And my ticket stub? It was in the breast pocket of my shirt. Plain, green, shaped like a razor blade; the sort of ticket you buy in strips at a fair. The word ONE printed on it, nothing else.

A shadow passed on the other side of the door, the sound and light muted by the glass to early twilight. Outside, birds sang, sunlight dappled the tree-lined sidewalk, people were out for their afternoon strolls with spouses, dogs, children. But like the man in the row ahead of mine, and all the patrons who did not see me, the sidewalk, and everything outside the theater, seemed impossibly distant.

I found that, despite my confusion, my anxiety, even my dread, I didn't have the slightest desire to leave.

I took my time getting back to the theater. In the dim light of the corridor the posters frowned back at me like the scions of a degraded heredity. I could even make out the creases and water stains and age freckles on them—Peoples never changed the posters, only rotated them, so that a different one appeared under the "Coming Soon" placard every few weeks. The restroom was empty—I tried all the stalls—as was theater 1, theater 2's mirror image. The patrons, I thought, have no reflection. I climbed the stairs to theater 3, whose advanced state of deterioration made me think that it had not been used for years, this though I was certain I had seen a film there just the week before. I cast a quick glance around the dusty seats and flaking ceiling before retreating to the narrow upstairs lobby.

It occurred to me then that I had never looked for a door to the projection booths. There might be several such doors, or just one, leading to a network of corridors and ladders and staircases inside the thin walls, like tunnels in an ant-farm. I had the vague idea that, if I could find this door, and bang on it, as I had on the box-office window, the noise would rouse the dozing projectionist, and he would release us from our limbo. But there was no door anywhere in the upstairs lobby besides the two leading to theater 3. Nor did I find any such door on the floor below.

Meanwhile in theater 2 nothing had changed. The same white heads were gathered in silent devotion, the coral pink still swirled on the screen, and the second movement of the Rachmaninoff concerto still quietly ebbed and flowed from the speakers. I had not been gone so long, then. But more: I was almost certain that the music had picked up again from the moment I left the theater. It was an impetus for me to retake my original seat—my customary seat, I should say: a seat I did not have to share, as in the upscale revival houses, with the ghost of some wealthy donor, in a mausoleum where the patrons are buried sitting.

Again I waited out the movement; and this time, when it ended, the audience members came to life. They coughed and cleared their throats, and one gentleman blew his nose. There was a bit of creaking and rustling in those old theater chairs before the third movement began, as I fully expected it would, *Allegro*, and louder again than the second.

By now I understood, or believed I understood, that I had not arrived early for a show yet to begin, but late for a performance already in progress. And I have no doubt that everything I say from this point forward will be blamed on a hyperactive fancy, and my tale combed for clues—the pocket watch, the effete and slightly pedantic language of the telling, the penchant for wiling away afternoons in old theaters, watching even older films—to prove me neurotic, eccentric, unreliable. But with the commencement of the third movement I found myself listening, really listening, for the first time, as though the mystery of the theater were hidden inside the music, whose familiarity had somehow rendered it mysterious. Perhaps it was because, as my attention drifted from the main current of the melody, it was drawn to the myriad eddies and pools I had habitually overlooked—

eddies and pools that now seemed to find their visual analog in the coral-pink swirls on the screen. Staring into them, as into the smoky glass of a crystal ball, I began to believe that I, too, could see. First the conductor at his podium, waving his fists at the orchestra, like a ship captain upon a bowsprit gesturing at a tumultuous sea; then the pianist, a cadaverous Slav with monstrous hands and a drawn, somber, skull-like face, sitting in the attitude of a sphinx for a small eternity. I could just make out the bows of the strings, all sawing away in unison. With the vision, the music sounded with a depth and clarity I could never remember hearing before; and as the movement drew on, alternating between ebullient dance and aching ballad, the vision in turn sharpened, to the point that it was difficult to remember, or to believe, that what I was watching *had to be* a projected image: the conductor, the piano, the orchestra from first violin to tympani, were as plainly visible to me as the wispy hairs on the back of the neck of the woman sitting two rows ahead of mine, as the clasp of her necklace, as the uneven hemming of her neckline. By the time the ballad returned in its bold, glorious, final variation, orchestra and piano joining to consummate that longing latent in the melody, there was no longer any doubt in my mind that I was witnessing, by whatever miracle, a live performance.

My fellow patrons were unable to restrain their applause until the final chord had quite rung out. A few had already risen to their feet. One clapped with a sort of serene dedication; another in sets of three, like a dog lapping water; another, still seated, shouted "bravo" through cupped hands. I myself started to applaud, quietly at first, so as not to draw attention, but with growing conviction the longer the applause went on. When in Rome, as they say. But this was hardly Rome, and I was no expatriate. I was not adopting foreign customs for the sake of keeping up appearances. No: I was belatedly learning my native ones.

Clapping, I remembered a debate with a friend some years before, in which I defended people's right to applaud at the end of a movie. He had argued that, without the artist present, applause was pointless; it was like applauding a painting in a museum. I countered that the applause was not necessarily intended as adulation of the (absent) artist, but was rather an acknowledgement of collective satisfaction on the part of the audience, and was hence a purer, more democratic form of appreciation. What's more—and this I asserted in the absence of any evidence—it had once been common to applaud at movies; that people no longer did was just one more sign of the unraveling of contemporary society. Well, this afternoon I felt my words come back to haunt me; for our applause was clearly directed at *something* beyond ourselves. I was reminded of my experience watching silent films when a pianist is present to accompany the screening. But in such cases, the applause is clearly directed at him, not at the film. I was reminded, too, of those epics like *Doctor Zhivago* that feature an orchestral overture. When the curtain opens, it is just possible to imagine that the flat surface on which the photoplay is projected is actually a window, opening onto a living scene. I remembered the moment in that film when the peasants throw open the door of a freight car in which they are traveling to find it entirely covered with ice. One breaks the ice with a stick, and the whole screen, a curtain of ice, shatters to reveal the Russian countryside.

This analogy, however, was still inadequate to what I was experiencing. I knew that *Zhivago* was a sophisticated illusion. But I could not shake the idea that the musicians I had conjured out of the pink haze were anything but living, breathing persons, sharing the same time and space as me. Clearly, my fellow patrons, whose applause petered and swelled as the principals returned to the stage for further adulation, were similarly convinced.

As it turned out, our appreciation was sufficient, and sufficiently directed at the pianist, to warrant a solo encore. When one of the standing patrons did not retake his seat, he was hailed with a "Down in front, please!" which was in turn answered with a loud "Shhhh!" A fidgety silence ensued. I watched the pianist's hands leap about the keyboard, his shoulders hunched in exquisite concentration, while the members of the orchestra looked on from their chairs. It was an exuberant few minutes, likely also Rachmaninoff—I am better acquainted with the orchestral works—and, when it concluded, was feted with the same billowing applause. This time I abandoned all reserve; I jumped to my feet and clapped my hands raw, shouted bravo, bravo, bravo. There followed a half-dozen curtain calls: the gaunt frame of the pianist, his drawn face not quite smiling; the stockier figure of the conductor beside him, bright and cherubic; and the members of the orchestra who had stood to join in the applause, the strings all clapping with bows in hand.

It was all so persuasive and well-intentioned that, when the moment at last arrived that a woman marched up to the stage and thrust a huge bouquet over its lip, I was hardly surprised to see the pianist step forward to receive it; to see his hand briefly join hers in a cordial shake; to see the flowers reappear above us, more dazzling in his arms than they had been in hers. I felt, not like someone who has just witnessed a miraculous, phantasmagorical exchange, but like someone observing the customs of a culture from which he has become estranged.

As the applause died down, the principals failed to return, the orchestra left in a drove, and the image sank back into the coral-pink haze, like a giant prop on casters slowly drawn into a cloud of theater smoke. The other patrons gathered their belongings, couples murmuring to each other. Leaving, they did not march up the aisle, as I expected they would, but rather hobbled in muttering train toward the front of the theater. There was an exit to the right of the stage, under a little green sign. I had noticed it before, of course, but had never seen anyone use it, and had come to assume it was reserved for emergencies. And this may indeed have been the case. For as the patrons neared the screen, they seemed to shrink, as though through some exaggeration of perspective; and in its vicinity they grew translucent, dissolving one after another into the haze, as if they themselves were mere projections overcome by an excess of light. I waited for them to re-materialize beside the exit. When they failed to do so, I had to conform myself to their simple disappearance. They were beings of light and shadow, not flesh and blood, and I was alone in the theater, as, perhaps, I had been from the beginning.

Except, that is, for my imagined projectionist. Was he my Wizard of Oz, subtly managing the whole affair, sitting back there in the booth with a trove of suitable encores and holographic projectors, manufacturing the shadow-play for which I was the sole audience? And if so, where did it end? Perhaps the usher, too, was a projection, and the concessions operator, and the solitaire-player. Perhaps Peoples itself was a projection, requiring a certain amount of twilight to become visible, and only perceivable in daytime to the elect.

No one had arrived to sweep up popcorn kernels or eject lingering patrons. The house lights remained up, as they had during the whole performance. I glanced behind me to ensure that the theater was indeed vacant, and noticed again the window of the projection booth, like the empty socket of a mechanical eye. No light, no passing shadow suggested movement or life.

And yet, that pink haze.

Rising, I did not approach the screen again, but went directly to the lobby, past the empty usher's podium, past the dark concession stand, down the corridor lined with posters, in whose glass frames I saw the outline of my reflection appear and disappear.

SCARECROW

The blinds were still drawn over the box-office window. On the floor of the vestibule was a single playing card, face down. I remembered my watch, five to three, and the ticket stub, ONE, which I once again removed from my breast pocket. Only the ticket was no longer one, but many. My pocket was full of tickets, spilling out onto the floor as I removed them. My sleeves were full of tickets, too, and when I reached down the neck of my shirt, I found more, and yet more. And I could feel myself diminishing with each fistful, as if I were no more than a scarecrow with tickets for straw, unstuffing and strewing myself about the vestibule floor while my body, such as it was, disappeared into the smoky light issuing through the glass door.

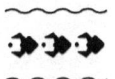

BURNING CHILD

AN ANODYNE

for Beverly Bronson

WE WENT OUT EARLY THAT EVENING, HOPING TO FIND A SEMI-SECLUDED table in this popular new Upper West Side Italian restaurant that did not take reservations. We were seated about halfway to the rear of a small, undivided, largely undecorated dining room, just beyond a quadrant of fading sunlight cast through the great glass wall facing out onto Amsterdam Avenue, checkered with the usual flattering reviews. Our timing was perfect: on returning from the restroom, I noticed that a crowd of prospective diners had assembled at the door. But when the maître d' struggled to seat a bickering family—two sets of in-laws, their respective children, and the couple's only child—he resolved to extend the table directly beside ours to seat six (seven, if you included the child). We effectively became the eighth and ninth adjuncts of their party. At least they had the good sense to seat the child at the table's far end, where it presided over our meals like a tiny patriarch.

We shared a chicory salad and a basket of bread. Sopping oil and vinegar from a shallow bowl, we worked leisurely through our entrees (ravioli, gnocchi) and first glasses of wine (dolcetto). We hardly spoke, our silence that comfortable plateau on which all successful relationships eventually settle, and which this evening achieved the additional sedentary euphoria that comes with alcohol and overeating. Contemplation of money well spent. A moment of catered-to satiety. For the most part we managed to ignore our uninvited tablemates.

At some point the adult children had started a fight over how the husband, who worked all week, wanted to hang around the apartment on weekends, while the wife, who spent the week at home with the child, used the weekends to make elaborate plans. This dilemma was presented as irreconcilable and life-shattering. The in-laws, who quite naturally got along better with each other than with their complement's children, agreed that the son and daughter should have "free agency" to do whatever he or she liked on weekends *individually*. They suggested this is what had made their own marriages fruitful, or at least long-lived. Then they all went back to picking at the family platter of rolled cold cuts and baked eggplant and cannellini and shrimp. The in-laws closest to us sipped sparkling wine and commented on how delicious our entrees looked. I liked them considerably more than their children; but then it is easy to admire senior citizens from a distance.

Then the fire started. I didn't see how. I was facing the rear of the dining room: the wine rack stacked neatly with bottles to the molded tin ceiling, the clear plastic mudflap that hung over the doorway to the restrooms and kitchen. I heard a clatter of dishes and the short, sharp cry of a child, neither louder than one would expect in a busy

Manhattan eatery. But these sounds, when extraordinary, are never distinguished by their volume: they are felt directly in the blood, like panic in a crowd. In truth, it's possible it wasn't the sound that moved me, but rather the lull directly after. Diners absorbed in the affair went silent, the room went still, and this might have given the sound a kind of retroactive gravity. I watched my wife lower her wine glass and raise her chin. These gestures carried enormous significance for me, if as yet no concrete meaning.

Perhaps the old man sitting next to me noticed something similar in his own spouse's gestures or expression, because he slid his chair out abruptly. He was still holding his glass of sparkling wine. For a moment it occurred to me that we were interlopers at a wedding celebration. The best man, I imagined, was about to propose a toast. So I, too, pushed out my chair.

The child—not the one at "our" table, but the one who had started on fire—had still not caught my attention. Instead, I watched the strange woman rise from a window table, grab a little girl's arm, and drag her toward the door. A few sparks and ashes moiled behind them, as when sap pops in a campfire; and the little girl, whose feet could not keep pace with the woman's, seemed carried on the draft. The woman spun around and hoisted the girl in her arms, clasping her to her body, and from the doorway confronted the commotion at the table. It was only then, in order to discover the object of *her* gaze, that I shifted my attention to the burning child.

Though I saw it, my mind did not immediately register that the child was on fire. Prejudiced by the look of the distraught mother, what I saw was a man beating a child, light and smoke trailing his striking hand, as from a juggler's torch. I was reminded of those hibachi places where the cooks light their grills on fire and make choochoo trains out of onions while families applaud. This child was a toddler, younger than the girl in the woman's arms. My impression was that the woman's horror was not at the fire, but at this monster flogging his child in the middle of a crowded restaurant, in our city's child-friendliest neighborhood.

The eleven o'clock news would report that the fire had started when the child knocked over a mood candle, and one of those polyester napkins went up like a hill of gunpowder. I remember our waiter lighting such a candle on our table when the dining room had grown dim enough. The papers the next morning would parrot this explanation. But my question was: who described this sequence of events to the news reporter? The mother? The father? The child's terrified sister? Who knew whether the candle started the blaze at all?

I now suspect that a burning napkin started the child's outfit on fire, sleeve-first, and that the outfit burned as well or better than the napkin. But at the time, because the napkin the father used to beat the child was itself on fire, I had the ridiculous impression that the father was trying to put out the burning napkin on the child's garment.

Whatever the order of events, the operative elements of the scene were as follows: desperate father beating burning child with burning napkin.

I turned the full power of my attention on the child. I could not tell its sex, as I could with what I presumed was its sister. It was dressed androgynously, strapped into one of those high chairs. Besides, it was on fire. One does not speculate about the sex of burning things; one tries to put them out. What amazed me, however, was that the child was not crying—at least, not yet. Nor did it look at its desperate, wailing father. It just stared straight ahead, kicking its little feet and waving its arms. This was what it was doing when the fire spread to its hair.

It didn't have much hair, of course. Its hair was of that fine, wispy kind you sometimes find on the outside of an egg, and as such I expected it to flare, singe briefly, and with a few more slaps of the napkin, go out. The father had finally abandoned the burning napkin for his bare hands—one on either side of the tiny skull—but no, this child was a Roman candle. It might have been the most flammable child in the world.

The father had by this time half-risen from his chair, and he stood perched over the burning child as if it were an object of worship, an idol whose veneration required its destruction. Then a glass shattered behind me, ending the preternatural quiet which, a moment before, had engulfed the restaurant; two women shrieked in rapid succession as if the one had cued the other, and one of the in-laws said, quite audibly, "Oh, Jesus. Oh, oh, God." A couple of people actually ran out of the restaurant, knocking the mother-daughter tableau (who were still standing in the doorway) into the coat rack. The child's mother seemed hardly to notice. Having realized that it was no longer the child's garment that burned, but the child itself, she set to wailing in the ear of its sibling, whom she still held clasped tightly in her arms, the more tightly, it seemed, the harder its sibling burned, as if these two actions shared an intimate, mysterious connection.

Then began the interventions into the family's affairs, as teams of waiters with their undecipherable accents formed ad hoc bucket brigades, dumping pitchersful of water onto child and father alike, in a kind of rehearsed clumsiness. The doused father continued to beat his child; but in his impotence to stop the conflagration from spreading to the toddler as a whole, he wept, and crumpled like paper in a hearth, and his beating became something closer to patting, or stroking. As for the child, neither fire nor water could elicit a sound, though it did writhe in its roiling shroud of flame, wearing a crown of flames upon its head, strapped to that throne which I could only imagine before too long would also begin to burn.

After seven or eight pitchers it became clear that this approach was as bankrupt as the father's. The water-bearing teams were followed by a mad little cook with a fire extinguisher. He reared up before the child, the nozzle pointed down over its skull, and squeezed the lever. The child was engulfed in a foamy white cataract. I somewhat absurdly began to fear that it would suffocate. And perhaps the cook was seized with a similar anxiety, or perhaps he just thought the fire was out, because he released the lever and withdrew the nozzle—only to see the flames spring back with redoubled fury.

Three times the cook squeezed the lever of the fire extinguisher, each time for a longer interval, shaking the whole contraption like a giant can of whipped cream. Three times the flames rebuffed him. And now entered the ostensible hero of the hour, a waiter brandishing a broad square rug, its corners flapping like the wings of a manta ray as he sprinted across the dining room. From his bearing and obvious authority I presumed he was the headwaiter. He tackled child and stool together, somehow managing to avoid the father. The glassware and china went crashing to the floor. This seemed to give the father a second wind, for with sudden vehemence he pounced on the rug beside the headwaiter, and together they commenced beating on it, looking for all the world like infants themselves. Jets of fire and great puffs of smoke shot out beneath them. My gaze cut left to right; everyone in the vicinity of the debacle was standing, as if to deliver an ovation. And I realized that I, too, had stood, although I could not remember doing so. With the exception of the father and the waitstaff (who had squadded up to cheer the headwaiter on) we all remained riveted in our places, as though we expected to be served when it was all over.

I haven't mentioned the smell. It was rank and overwhelming. Late that night, even after I had showered several times, the smell still lingered, as it would for some days after.

We knew we were in trouble when the rug began to burn, sending chugging masses of black smoke to curl along the ceiling. And because of the tin clanging of the alarm, or because the burning child was out of sight, the evacuation of the restaurant now began in earnest. Many who had been standing nearest to the table jostled for the door, some covering their heads with coats, as if they wished to conceal their identities. The mother-daughter was thrust bodily onto the sidewalk by this wave of evacuees. Diners ran to and fro pointlessly, some shouting into cell phones. A couple of young men actually found the belated wherewithal to charge forward with their own coats, or with other people's coats, and tackle the rug/ bewildered father/ headwaiter/ burning child. Those who had neither participated in the initial rush for the door, nor attempted to come to the aid of the burning child, began to dribble out, each alone, caught between the beginning of a threat to their own safety and a spectacle which they quite naturally desired to witness to its end. They stepped dreamily, and with a sort of borrowed dignity, holding their belongings out before them and orbiting the smoldering pile of men and fabric.

For a moment those of us who remained—those of us who were unable to tear ourselves away—were unsure whether the most recent efforts to smother the child were having the desired effect. Then all at once the coats went up like tinder, forcing the unidentified Samaritans, the headwaiter, and finally the father from the pile. As they stumbled back, I noticed that the headwaiter took the father by the elbow in a gesture at once solicitous and proprietary.

And then the siren, filling the spaces between the clanging of the alarm and the shouting patrons. It grew louder, until it drowned out every other sound, and became another silence. Could it be that this child had become an authentic city event, that it could by itself call out an entire ladder company? The station was right around the corner, the firefighters could have run here faster, carrying extinguishers of their own. But then the siren plummeted and ceased, and the red and chrome hull of the fire truck appeared in the window, toy-bright, blotting out the failed sun. My heart leapt, actually leapt: I thought, Here at last is the answer! I could see dials and meters and valves, like on the inside of a submarine; and in the cacophony I imagined I heard the ping of a submarine's radar.

There was a tug at my sleeve. It was my wife. I had never even looked around to verify she was still there. Her mouth moved quickly and emphatically. I touched my earlobe and furrowed my brow. She frowned and tugged harder.

"And the child?" I shouted.

And then our world became all breaking glass and jetting water as a phalanx of helmeted firefighters burst through the glass wall, pointing their hoses everywhere—at the bonfire of coats, the carpet, child: a fire suited for a bacchanal. The ceiling was lost in an inverted sea of smoke, and molten tin ran in rivulets down the walls. Water tore through the dining room, taking with it a pandemonium of tables and diners alike, obliterating the wine rack in a shower of glass. There was a traffic of plates and saucers in the air around us. I watched a leg of lamb turn in languid arcs before it landed somewhere beyond the plastic mudflap hanging over the kitchen door. A gob of what I later determined to be baked eggplant struck me on the forehead with the force of a bullet. When a firefighter finally escorted my wife and I outside, one of their heavy blankets thrown across our shoulders, the water had pooled up to our ankles.

We didn't go home immediately. But neither, as you might expect, did we stay to witness the outcome. The fire was brought under control, of course. We watched as the remaining diners were escorted out, looking for the heroic headwaiter, and for the father, who finally appeared on a stretcher, his raw hands dangling stiffly. For a few minutes there was a lull in the activity; I thought I saw a couple of firefighters stamping on the once-blazing mound with their big boots. How were they to know what precious gem was buried underneath that carpet? Another ambulance arrived, another police cruiser. And then someone must have told the firefighters how the blaze had gotten started, because a pair still wearing their helmets and heavy boots hurdled the sill and started peeling coats off that pile on the floor. That was our cue. The single heavy blanket around our shoulders forced us to walk in tandem. As we left, we scanned the crowd halfheartedly for the mother and sibling child.

The eleven o'clock news was a cipher, as were the early tabloids my wife dragged me to the newsstand for at six the next morning. There were half-page pictures of the family in their better days, the same ones in each paper, invariably accompanied by a short column of text running along the outside gutter, maybe three hundred words long. They mentioned the suspected genesis of the fire, the death of the child (aged one year three months, name not revealing of its sex), the treatment of the father for severe burns and several other diners for minor injuries and smoke inhalation. Three sources were quoted: the owner of the restaurant, a grieving relative (not a member of the immediate family), and a witness who had dined elsewhere. My wife folded the papers and threw them in the trash on the way home.

I don't dream about any of this. My wife does, relentlessly. Terrible dreams which she takes pains to describe to me in great detail immediately upon waking. In fact, she describes them in such detail, and so shortly after waking—waking me, sometimes, to have an audience before the narrative evaporates from her consciousness—that the next morning I am not always sure I didn't dream it. Maybe much of what I claim to have reported here, she dreamed. In one, the child burns helplessly, but happily, surrounded by golden flames like the Christ child's halo in a Medieval painting, and by a host of concerned onlookers, or acolytes, who comment dryly on the miracle of its unsinged flesh. In another, my wife stands inside the restaurant, empty and a shambles, upon a broad expanse of carpet, when a hand comes into the frame of her vision and turns the corner back. In some versions of this dream, the child stares unscarred at the tin ceiling, and though it lies rigid, she says that she expects it to smile and put a finger to its lips at any moment, as if it were all a trick. Other times it is but a charred skeleton that writhes. "And it *hisses*," she says. She dreams these false endings for both of us, unloading them upon me, until it seems like we *did* stay to see that pale fireman hump a roll of carpet to the sidewalk.

She doesn't believe me that I don't dream. She thinks I'm holding back. What I don't tell her is that when I walk around the neighborhood I sometimes imagine I see smoke coming out of every stroller I pass. Or that sometimes, when I see a child coming toward me holding its parent's hand, when it is still too far away for its features to have resolved, it seems to me disfigured. So many children, you could pave the streets with them, lay the foundations for every skyscraper and tenement. Why shouldn't one occasionally burst into flame? I think about that father helplessly beating a burning napkin against his child, who burned so stoically, and with such resolve, it might have burned for a hundred centuries, as long as the cores of planets, the hearts of stars. For all I know that little body might burn yet, a live coal glowing in its coffin, warming the ground around its grave to the very soles of the mourners' shoes. Child, why did you burn? In spite of all that was done for you, in spite of all our care and anguish and the mighty arm of the New York City firefighters?

THE HOTEL FIRE

*The menace of destruction is
always lurking in the inorganic world.*

LOTTE H. EISNER

1

THE HOTEL HAD BEEN ON FIRE FOR DAYS AND DAYS.

It was a Radisson or Hilton or some such thing, fifty stories tall, taking up a whole city block somewhere in the mid-fifties, a massive capital-H seen from the sky. It had a covered semicircular drive where brass-buttoned bellhops greeted you, and one of five identically-friendly clerks, though never the same one, would hail you from the counter as soon as you stepped through the revolving doors. The ground floor boasted two restaurants, three cafeterias, a lounge, an art gallery, a game arcade, and a souvenir shop. There were hundreds of staff, a dozen elevators, two thousand rooms, and thousands of guests.

At the beginning it seemed a fire like any other, and those of us who happened to be in the neighborhood on the first day paused like any other pedestrian to watch the gaggle of firefighters in heavy coats carrying axes or pike poles. Their trucks were parked crookedly along the avenue where yellow tape was stretched. We stayed just long enough to witness the flames leaping from a window fifteen stories up, to shudder at the precariousness of our lives, to mentally cross-examine ourselves about the electrical cords and outlets and stoves in our apartments, maybe to see the glittering cascades of glass as windows were punched out and the flames mellowed into billowing black cloud. The rest of us watched it on the news that night, a succession of five or six images compressed into fifteen seconds among the minute or two allotted to local events. No one was hurt. No word as to the cause of the blaze.

A couple of days later, when the hotel started burning again, we sat up and took notice. On the news, the fire trucks looked exactly the same as before.

In the days that followed, as the crowds around the hotel multiplied and the news and fire trucks became a near-constant presence, something of the future of the event could already be glimpsed. Almost immediately, the media stopped talking about fires in the plural, and began referring to a single, spreading fire, this though individual fires were extinguished before new ones broke out, and they began in seemingly unrelated parts of the building. The manager soon acquiesced—perhaps a single fire, no matter how prolonged, seemed to him less threatening than many—taking the opportunity to add that no guests were in danger, the situation was under control, and that the hotel would continue to go about its business with the same courtesy and efficiency for which it was justly renowned.

It was also during these formative weeks that the fire marshal stopped blaming careless guests and staff—the maid who tossed a lit cigarette into a tub of dirty linen; the Spanish socialite who left his hot pot plugged in; the errant bellboy's unwholesome fascination with his Zippo—and began suggesting foul play. The tabloids soon had their man: a latter-day Bolshevik, dressed in the trench coat and black fedora of a Cold War spy. But the foul-play thesis could not be sustained for very long, either. For by this time the guests and staff had already been interrogated and their backgrounds checked; several had been sacked for misdemeanors overlooked at the time they were hired, and several more were being held for deportation. In the face of questions from reporters, the marshal was forced to admit that investigators had not turned up a single shred of evidence pointing to arson. However, the marshal reasoned, since the cause of every fire left a trace, the only plausible explanation for the absence of said trace was the *presence* of a malign hand acting intentionally to erase it.

With no leads among the staff or registered guests, and despite the momentary absence of any fire, the city ordered an evacuation, which the police closely monitored, and the premises were searched from roof to cellar, room by room, in the company of the superintendent and his Brobdignagian ring of keys.

It was only after the fire marshal had given the all-clear sign, but before anyone had been readmitted to the hotel, that the fire broke out anew.

We couldn't blame them, the police and firefighters, the media, the manager, the mayor, the city as a whole, for wanting the fire to have some agent, some cause—something or someone you could point a finger at, give a name to, say, *There*, or, *He*. Nor were we ourselves immune, although our imaginations, free from practical considerations, tended toward the metaphysical and fantastic. A sort of Maxwell's demon, maliciously opening and closing dampers. A will-o'-the-wisp flashing gayly down empty hallways, seeding blazes in its wake. In those early days, in fugue from our lives proper, we had to amuse ourselves somehow, beyond watching the halting progress of the fire, and speculating about where it would strike next.

It was impossible to tell; its progress defied all logic. And no one knew this better than the firefighters themselves. If a fire was reported in, say, room 1116, rather than spreading to an adjacent room, or to that room's mirror image on a floor above or below, it might reappear in room 1692, or 510—to pull numbers out of a hat. With the careless guests/staff thesis quashed, and the foul-play thesis ridiculed, the firefighters turned their attention to the hotel's great circulatory system of heating and cooling ducts. Once it was agreed that the blaze was the product of a single slow-burning fire rather than a series of discrete successive ones, figuring out the method of transmission became paramount—if, that is, the firefighters hoped to reach the fire's ultimate cause, and extinguish it once and for all. Only such channels, it was reasoned, could carry sparks and burning material great distances across the hotel, to sow new and seemingly unconnected blazes, and supply them with the oxygen necessary to burn. In this sense, the fire could be said not so much to be spreading as reproducing itself, like a dandelion going to seed.

Those of us who believed the investigation had gotten off track in its search for criminals and negligents were relieved by the change of focus. Only later did it come to our attention that the ducts had been a locus of concern from the very first day. In fact, the air had been turned on and off, and vents and dampers opened and closed, according to the present location of the fire. Here was the problem: because of its size, the hotel was heated and cooled in segments that were, according to the superintendent, *entirely independent of each other.* Yet, if the fire was indeed moving via the ducts, it had managed to pass between these ostensibly discrete systems unimpeded. In fact, only desperation on the part of the new fire marshal—the old one had since resigned and joined our ranks outside the hotel, loitering in the vicinity of the news trucks—had turned the investigators' attention back to the system. And it was only when the building plans were revisited in the company of the superintendent that this furtive little man mumbled something to the effect that the plans before them were only the barest reflection of the reality of the hotel, and hardly representative of its actual ventilatory network.

Now the real investigation began. Experts were called in from every corner of the country: civil and structural engineers, captains of the heating and cooling industry, veteran contractors and fire investigators. Blueprints were unrolled, historical records unburied, old work orders uncovered and dusted off. For days the team pored over these documents, which were variously reported to be forged, contradictory, ambiguous, and incomplete. Another problem: the hotel had changed hands several times since its construction shortly after the end of World War II, with apparently unauthorized renovations carried out by successive owners and owning entities. As the dead ends multiplied, the coalition of experts began to fracture, bickering and throwing up their hands in frustration, calling the investigation a sham, a quixotic fantasy, a waste of taxpayers' money. The city, to its credit, dug in its heels. More documents were unearthed, previous superintendents and contractors subpoenaed; even simple day laborers were located and questioned—anyone who might be able to shed light on what increasingly appeared to be an endlessly complex network of capillaries honeycombing the building's walls. Debates broke out over whether extant documents or living memory could possibly do justice to the smoke-snorting behemoth that burned in fits and starts and calmly defied all attempts at rational explanation. Nor was our occasional fatalism undermined by the fantastic stories told by those workers the city had managed to track down, some of whom claimed to have been present at the hotel's initial construction. In one widely-reproduced interview, a Russian octogenarian responded to each question by shaking his head and jabbing a finger at the sky, as if to suggest that the hotel had not been built by human hands, but rather had descended from heaven.

In its desperation for results, the city consulted with a mathematician, an expert in probability, statistics, and chaos. His tenure on the payroll marks the nadir of the city's efforts to defeat the fire, and for many of us, at least in hindsight, the breaking-point of their credibility. He appeared one day out of the blue, an Austrian who had reputedly made and lost fortunes in Monaco before slinking back into the shadows of academe. He proclaimed that by submitting the sequence of rooms in which the fire appeared to a complex series of algorithms, he could determine, with a high degree of certainty, where it would strike next. Although we distrusted the mathematician—his Germanic darkness and nervous squint, the way he smiled wryly after each clipped phrase he uttered—we dearly wanted him to succeed. We wanted, that is, the elements, *time itself*, to submit, not to the half-measures of tea leaves and crystal balls, but to the sheer, raw force of the human intellect, which the mathematician, in his arrogance, represented to us. We felt sorry for each new fire marshal, condemned to fight a symptom rather than the disease. For the hotel fire was just that: a symptom of a deeper infection—a deeper *something*—and the marshal, a doctor condemned to prescribe skin cream for a fever rash.

The mathematician was given three chances, and then a fourth after he appealed to the marshal and mayor. Each attempt was accompanied by great drama. They tried, without success, to keep his choices secret. Once the news had circulated, we would pick up our belongings and migrate in the direction of the room, from busy avenue to quiet cross-street, or vice-versa, and then hold our breaths, our hands clasped together, staring up at the oracular window. With each failure—that is, with each report that the fire had begun elsewhere—a cry would go up. On what was to be his final attempt, the mathematician appeared to err magnificently, until he pointed out that the number of the room that did burn was a permutation of the one he had predicted. Moreover, he argued, the first two attempts had done little but give him a chance to calibrate his instrument, and each successive attempt was exponentially more likely to succeed. This argument might have befuddled the fire marshal and mayor, but it did little to restore the faith of rank-and-file firefighters, or the public. With his final and most spectacular failure, the mathematician came to be regarded as a charlatan, and the whole regrettable episode a cautionary tale in this tragedy that unfolded incrementally under our watchful eyes. It wasn't long before the mathematician, like the old fire marshal, joined our ranks, wearing a great sandwich-board covered with formulae and variously-sized question marks, and proclaiming to whoever would listen that the hotel fire was *a truly random process*, the first of its kind in nature, a mathematical anomaly, not to say impossibility, and that as such he had given up studying it and decided to worship it.

Of course, the mathematician wasn't the only one who gambled on the fire. There were dozens of pools, money changing hands with each new blaze. Nor was the gambling confined to the immediate vicinity of the hotel: some news reports estimated that tens of millions of dollars circulated daily through this upstart sector of the numbers-running industry. The vast majority of us, however, saw something far greater in the hotel fire than the momentary thrill of wagering a few dollars; and even as the mathematician dashed our last bit of faith in the fire's knowability, even as we were ready to join him and his sandwich-board chanting the end times, and to worship the hotel fire like Hollywood natives dancing in grass skirts, we were loath to abandon it to mere chance. We were stubborn for purpose, for meaning. In our desperation to find something commensurate with the fire, to explain why it would burn intermittently but unstoppably, we began inventing histories of infamy for guests past and present, a veritable rogues' gallery: foreign torturers seeking asylum, gangsters languishing under witness protection, insatiably lustful priests. We speculated about the atrocities that had been committed at the hotel, such transient spaces being always magnets for vice, the evil of countless unheralded deeds soaked into the blandest wallpaper, so that even the most virtuous of current guests, or at least the weaker-minded among them, became susceptible to intermittent possession, driving them to arson, or worse.

But even as we imagined these ridiculous scenarios we knew that the hotel was neither a haven for old criminals nor a hotbed for new ones. The hotel had not been built on a lake of fire, or on an old Indian or slave burial ground. There was no evil welling up from the soil of the past. There was no geometrically unfathomable system of ducts through which sparks could be carried hither and thither to every corner of the building, no strange little men, real, spiritual or metaphorical, no demons abstract or concrete. Above all, there was no structural flaw. But neither was it a question of the malign hand of an architect or builder. The hotel was the sum total of a thousand intentions, millions of tiny acts. It had no conscience, no memory, no power of reason; but it did have a destiny, which it enacted before our eyes. Or perhaps it had only a will—perhaps it was only will: pure, materialized will, whose mere exercise was self-consuming. For all we knew, all materials, all elements, were infused with just such an insidious latent life, a will predicating obsolescence, a kind of death-wish, which, when they were arranged just so, and in such-and-such combination, became manifest. So it was said many years earlier about the Bronx: *The Bronx is burning*. A simple declaration in the present continuous tense, without agent or end. But while it might be said that this statement deliberately concealed a malign hand, in the case of the hotel fire it was apt.

2

In time, the hotel corporation came to realize that the fire was more recognizable than the red neon corporate logo which flashed now amid a perpetual haze from the building's penultimate, windowless floor. For as the fire became less and less a news item for city residents, and as the firefighters became at once a near-invisible presence at the scene and fodder for late night talk show hosts' monologues, so it simultaneously became a must-see attraction for tourists. Pilots pointed to the smoke as they flew over the island on takeoff and landing. Tour buses changed their routes to pass it. Before long, it was as recognizable a sight as the Empire State Building's chameleonic cupola, and even made it into the quirkier tour books, where it came to be referred to, simply, as The Burning Hotel.

Once upon a time, you could have looked up at the buildings surrounding the hotel and witnessed the eerie spectacle of hundreds upon hundreds of office workers gazing out on the fire in groups of two and three from their office windows, frozen there, like mannequins. But as the fire became for residents and commuters less a spectacle than a nuisance, their numbers diminished. Altercations arose as area workers tried to hack a path through our always-swelling numbers in order to gain their commute. It was little use trying to explain to them that our numbers had swelled not with the faithful, but with tourists from Europe and Australia on their way between Fifth Avenue and Times Square, and families in for the day from Jersey, snapping pictures and sitting children on their shoulders, like the hotel fire was a parade. To the commuters we were all the same, legitimate targets for their ire, which we felt might have been more profitably directed at their places of employment. They told us to get lives. What use was it telling them that this was precisely what we had done?

As for the tourists who stayed at the hotel, they soon seemed as accustomed to the fire as the workers. No longer did they call the front desk in a panic to report smoke curling out of the ice machine, or the jack-o-lantern glow around a nearby door. No longer did maids have to suffer the indignity of being corralled by near-naked foreign men, shouting in broken English that their rooms were ablaze. No longer, that is, could anyone claim that they didn't know what they were getting into: the occasional, piecemeal evacuations, more a formality; the perpetual smell of smoke. Anyway, they knew a bargain when they saw one. Shortly after the fire had started, room rates slumped. There was no need for the fire code to be enforced for the hotel to glimpse ruin. The pressure came not from the city—not surprising, given the hotel's clout with the latter's various, interlocking political machines—but from corporate headquarters. The embarrassment of the hospitality industry, they called it. The manager would not mention the fire, but defended his decision to drop rates as an emergency measure. We believed he was smarter than his superiors gave him credit for, and we were hardly surprised when the hotel began to emerge from its smouldering chrysalis as the great, blazing butterfly we always knew it to be. For even as the hotel slipped deeper into the red, registration rebounded to near pre-fire levels. From a guest's perspective, this made eminent sense: with over two thousand rooms, the probability of one's room catching fire (the average frequency of a "new" fire being about twice the length of an average stay) was less than 0.1%. The chance of being in one's room the moment the fire broke out was even less, and of burning to death as a result, less still. On the other hand, as the staff never tired of pointing out, the chance of being mugged or shot on the city's mean streets was considerably higher. Never mind that the current level of meanness of the city's streets was open to debate, or that (as a reporter later revealed) the comparison turned out to be statistically challenged. Savvy consumers got the message, and learned to take the fire in stride. For really, what was a minuscule chance of burning to death measured against the opportunity to stay in one of Manhattan's most elegant midtown hotels at a fraction of the cost of its competitors?

Registration soared, and rates followed. The hotel was booked solid for months. Suddenly, it was no longer just a spectacle to be gawked at, but an event to be experienced. The fire gave guests an authentic feeling of danger; for who was to say it wasn't your room that would go up in flames this time? Once again, the quirkier tour books quickly updated their New York entries, expanding the hotel's original listing under "Accommodations," and this time even their more conservative competitors followed suit. The Burning Hotel, as one pun-happy guide put it, was now "the hottest three-night-stand in town."

As for why the hotel was so slow to capitalize on its new popularity, most of us blamed the risk-averse culture of the corporation, which, it must be admitted, had helped to create, and had much at stake in, the hotel's reputation for courtesy and efficiency. So we could not help but see the hand of the manager at work again when they sacked most of the marketing division and hired a cabal of twentysomethings, who immediately set about making over the hotel in order to take advantage of its incendiary architecture. The first thing they did was to paint a ring of flames around the lobby, and down the halls of every floor, and around the outside of the building three stories up. Soon the bars were serving drinks with variations on the "burning" theme, and the kitchens became famous for their hot wings and "sizzlers" (both of which were really quite bland). Clerks were encouraged to speak with more "fire" by, say, occasionally insulting guests, disparaging their dress or hair, or using foul language. Maids and bellboys undid the top buttons of their prison-orange uniforms, and staff were given whistles, and trained to denounce slacking coworkers by blowing the whistles and shouting, "Fire!" They were encouraged, too, after the slogan of the most recent ad campaign, to use the phrase "put a little spark" into every available circumstance, or to create such circumstances when they did not exist.

Area residents, in the meantime, had organized around the supposed threat that the fire represented to their community—not out of fear that the fire would spread to their residences, but because the drain on equipment and manpower implied by the constant presence of firefighters around the hotel left them vulnerable. God forbid, they said, that a fire should break out a block away from the hotel, for whoever lived there would surely burn to death while the fire trucks didn't budge and the firefighters stood around looking up at the hotel windows like birdwatchers. It was clear that the community, or at least its most vocal members, regarded the fire as a promotional stunt, not far removed from the theories of the vibrant conspiracy culture that had grown up around the hotel's new profitability. Some simply refused to believe that the fire department was so incompetent as to be unable to extinguish the fire for months on end. And if not incompetent, then it must be either deliberately negligent, or criminally engaged; there was no other possibility. When we pointed to the period before the hotel came to recognize the fire as an asset, the conspiracy theorists agreed that the first phase of the fire might have been outside the hotel's control, but its later profitability revealed a clear economic imperative. Given its responsibility to shareholder interests, they said, the corporation simply could not afford to let the fire fizzle.

The community pressured the city for a general evacuation, which, they claimed, would put an end to "this fire nonsense" once and for all. It might have been true that the purported negligence of the fire department left the community vulnerable, and that a tragedy, given these circumstances, was inevitable. But somehow, nobody seemed to realize that that the most likely site for the tragedy was the hotel itself. So it was that an old German couple, about whom little was known and less remembered, was burned alive as they slept in room 2356 at the end of the fire's fourth month. A few weeks later, three young French artists, who were reputed to have said that dying in the burning hotel would turn their lives into transcendent, monumental works of art, got their wishes, if not their concomitant fame, though photos of their snarled, charred corpses did briefly circulate the web. Finally, and most egregiously, a young couple from Nebraska and their two children burned to death huddled together in their bathroom on the third floor. There were the usual inquiries, hearings, post-mortems, protests, histrionics from city councilmembers, denunciations of the power of big money to corrupt politics, etc., etc. Tourists were exhorted to exercise personal responsibility for the risk of staying at The Burning Hotel. But even as the deaths mounted—or possibly because they did—the hotel became that much more a juggernaut, not so much outside the city's control as an image of the city itself.

Although the hotel lost room after room in its near-daily fires, even after several months' burning, the number of rooms lost amounted to less than 5% of the total. At this rate, the hotel would take a full five years to "burn to the ground," assuming that it did absolutely nothing to remediate the burnt portions of its property. There was a brief dip in new registrants, though whether it was due to the building's beginning to resemble a housing project—all those boarded-up sockets visible from the street, like so many missing teeth in the corporate smile—or whether people remained a little spooked by "Nebraska" (as the event came to be known in marketing circles), was unclear. Regardless, the mini-slump was the opportunity one of the young marketing geniuses behind the hotel's original makeover had been waiting for. The greatest tragedy, he announced, would be for the hotel's popularity to run its course before the fire had. His revelation was to restore each burned-out room according to a different theme or vision, utilizing the talents of both famous designers and lesser-known, local artists. Supporting the local arts economy would not only give the hotel street cred, he argued, but improve its image as a good corporate citizen in the wake of "Nebraska." Finally, the *pièce de résistance* of each renovation would be its eclectic window, which would simultaneously memorialize the earlier burning *and* announce the identity of the designer. Portholes, loopholes, deadlights—nothing was judged too eccentric. In fact, the young ad-man's entire vision amounted to a broadside against the hotel's perceived staid uniformity, which, he argued, was incompatible with its new image. As for the guests who stayed in these rooms, they would also be touched by the previous fire. It would be as if they, too, had burned at some time in the past, and were living out a glimpsed future life, with all the possibilities and freedom that entailed.

The plan implied an enormous outlay of capital, of course—not just in construction, but design and marketing as well. But from the first completed renovation, it turned out to be amply justified. Even at the new rooms' exorbitant rates, demand was unprecedented, and the guests who stayed there became instant celebrities. In this way, several minor midwestern capitalists and the dignitaries of tiny, insincere nations enjoyed their moments in the sun; and although we had no idea who they were, when they came to their windows to wave, we could at least point to them and say, He's staying in the Ralph Lauren room, or the Keith Haring room, or what have you. It was true that some ordinary folks squandered their life savings for an opportunity to stay a night in a room attributed to some lesser-known designer. But by and large the renovations were advertised to the already-celebrity, for whom the once-unhip hotel had become a destination, and who were spotted in its main lounge with increasing frequency.

Although the conspiracy theories lost some traction after "Nebraska"—few believed that firefighters would murder a family in cold blood—they soon resurfaced in mutated form. Why, theorists now asked, would firefighters remain day after day in the vicinity of a fire they seemed unable to defeat? In return, we asked how it would have looked had they simply pulled up stakes and retreated to their stations. We supposed they continued fighting the fire for no other reason than because they were firefighters, it was their profession, and theirs was not to question why, etc. We wondered if the theorists had ever bothered to look at their faces: the stony, grizzled, soot-caked faces lining the sidewalks where the fire companies were encamped. They would enter the building in gangs of three and four, clopping along like drafthorses in their coats and helmets, carrying their axes and Halligan bars, passing similar-sized groups of tourists on their way out, who chatted and laughed, and swung their purses in great arcs, and perhaps paused to snap a picture with their phones of those grim, determined men moving off to some unspecified point in the hotel where fire had been reported. It was what they had paid for: the excitement of the fire brigade passing at arm's reach; the epiphenomena of a tragedy that might at any moment be their own, enjoyed from the relative safety of probability.

Though our role was much more modest, like the firefighters we were committed to seeing the fire through to the end. We watched it as one watches a turbulent sea dismantling a vessel just beyond the surf, hapless to approach, even as the noise of its doomed passengers gusts ashore. We imagined, that is, that we were tending to a being terminally ill, yet divine. Our inability to imagine an end made us only that much more certain that it would come. So we thought of ailing sagueros, and shot elephants, and harpooned whales, and we waited for the equivalent of the gory death-spout, half-believing the behemoth would expire with a fantastic groan, yet knowing all the

73

while that it was we who would emit that final cry; that the only sound the hotel would make was that of its own falling, of half a century's coagulated labor crumbling to the earth.

3

The hotel had been on fire for days and days, but one day it happened that the fire no longer burned as a succession of discrete rooms, but began burning in swathes of three and four rooms together, and then in whole wings and floors. It happened almost overnight, the way a village of thatched roofs may become an inferno from a single small blaze with a sudden change in the direction of the wind. In this case, the wind—at least the most memorable event to whose proximity in time we could ascribe the sort of necessity that the hotel fire inspired—was the announcement that the hotel, tired of the generic "burning" epithet, would henceforth be known as The Hotel Prometheus. It was like the name a condemned man shouts, his or his general's or his cause's, the moment before the commander of the firing squad lowers his sword.

The signs were there for anyone to read, although more legible, of course, in hindsight. Over the preceding months the reception area had taken on a gaudy, faux-Egyptian cast worthy of Las Vegas, with torches lighting the way to the bar and elevators, and festooning the walls of the lounge. Drinks sizzled; shots were lit; fondue came back in style; kitchens were relocated to where the cooking fires could be easily observed by diners. In the arcade, the shuffleboard pokers were painted black, and bocce was played on hot coals. On occasion, the wooden balls exploded. Bellboys became hellboys, and then imps, wore crowns of flame; and maids, now succubi, were themselves set ablaze—actual flaming maids, running down the halls carrying bundles of burning linen. The concierge was perpetually covered in soot.

To keep the smoke to a bearable maximum—enough, that is, for a haze to persist in the halls, and for the occasional ambient cough from a guest—an elaborate new exhaust system was installed. Occasional coughs were played over hidden loudspeakers, too, and a constant, near-inaudible crackle, as of crickets in the countryside, accompanied guests wherever they went. As for the manager, he took on the role of the Devil himself. We could almost see his henchmen shoveling bills into an oven, like firemen used to coal; for the hotel grew only more profitable the nearer it approached its auto-da-fe.

The turn in the fire was first reported by a "nomad," that is, one who roamed around the block, rather than settling on a particular street or avenue, as the majority of us had done. He informed us that three fires were burning simultaneously on three different sides of the building. This in itself was not so alarming; simultaneous fires had broken out in different parts of the hotel before. But when they persisted, and then spread, a thrill ran through us. Soon the south side of the hotel was showing six, and then seven, and then ten windows all spitting flames like dragons' gullets. The great façade was a checkerboard of fires. The end had begun.

There were dozens if not hundreds of new firefighters on the scene, men and women we no longer recognized, and convoys of hook and ladder trucks jammed up the streets, their spinning lights competing with the glow of the blaze. No matter how many reinforcements they brought—and within a day the whole force seemed to have converged there—they were not enough to address the extant fires, let alone their growth, as what one marshal had described as a slow-motion game of whack-a-mole exploded into anarchy. Signals got crossed; already-exhausted firefighters fanned out through the hotel, sprinting up and down distant stairwells, where they were left alone to die smothered and cremated in nameless wings. Others collapsed and were carried out of the building by their comrades, deposited along the sidewalks in heaps. Theirs were the black faces greedily sucking oxygen from masks passed among colonies of prone bodies, as the panoply of jagged ladders multiplied and the bulging canvas anacondas crossed thick as viscera and the streets ran like rivers and the guests intrepid or insane continued to enter and exit and the hotel continued to profit and to burn.

Finally the city called a general evacuation, over the protests of the manager and the board of trustees, who held that the situation was not so dire as it appeared, little worse, in fact, than it had been for the preceding year, certainly not bad enough to justify an evacuation, particularly given what many of the guests had paid to stay there. The guests, they maintained, were adequate arbiters of their own safety, and evacuating the hotel now would be as good as shuttering it once and for all. It was rumored that the hotel encouraged their guests to defy the city's orders, but that hardly seemed necessary. People were still trying to check in, sensing that it would be their last opportunity to stay there, confounded by the many guests who refused to check out. Some had no doubt gone there specifically to self-immolate, determined to be among the elect who perished with the hotel. They barred their doors; they hid inside their rooms; they assumed traditional poses of non-resistance when the firefighters broke in, at great personal risk, to haul them away. Some fought tooth-and-nail with their would-be saviors. Others proved unrescuable: locked away in regions of the hotel made inaccessible by the fire, they waved handkerchiefs out their windows, not to signify their desire to be saved, but to announce their presence to us. And they were unsaveable, too, from the great ladders violating the sky in staggered combination, a sky so blue the earth seemed peeled, the firefighters black as birds against it, smoke wafting around them like Wagnerian mist, trying to keep their balance high atop the heads of those crooked pins, only to attempt to rescue those determined not to be, unable either to pull them out or persuade them in arguments shouted over a few feet of empty space and the siren-pulses far below, and sometimes with guests who started burning even before the argument had been abandoned.

There were those who changed their minds too late, or seemed to. One guest made a rope of knotted linens and tried to shimmy down from the eleventh floor. Not only did the rope stretch only halfway to the ground, but a new conflagration began on a floor below. He had already climbed halfway down when the rope caught fire beneath him, and was unable to reach his window again before the flames overtook him. He burned where he hung. When he fell, it was because the rope had burned through, and the burning linen became his shroud, flapping like a sail wrapped around a body cast into the sea. There were many such grisly, fantastic scenes. And there were many who simply jumped.

In time the firefighters themselves were no longer allowed inside. The ones who had not returned were presumed dead, and the guests who had refused to evacuate, or who otherwise could not be accounted for, who could no longer be seen in their windows blowing kisses and waving handkerchiefs, were also given up for lost. The building itself was judged dangerously close to collapse; the crowds were pushed back onto the surrounding blocks. The bedraggled firefighters joined our ranks, exposed their stout hearts buried under their coats, their helmets cradled under their arms. They were smoked to nought but sweat and grizzle, and shadows burned under their eyes; their oxygen tanks were empty; the hydrants had run dry, like the rivers drunk by Cyrus's armies on the march from Persia. Together, we watched as Gideons Bibles burned by the thousands, together with thousands of Impressionist reproductions. Bars of individually-wrapped soap burned, and tiny bottles of shampoo and conditioner became so many candles. Courtesy hangers and ironing boards, comforters and single-serve bags of Colombian coffee; even the sprinkler heads must have burned, sputteringly at first, and then melted and run together with the ice machines and exploded pop cans and room-service trays, fused into metalplasticwood, while the hotel threw up vast quantities of smoke and ash, like a child tossing handfuls of sand at the beach. It blazed, a skyscraper of fire, making fuel out of its own destruction, and so burning more fiercely with each passing moment, a Manhattan Vesuvius threatening to take along with it not only the city block it occupied, but the whole damned island.

But the promise of eternal fire was, as always, an illusion. It burned this way for just three days, turning the air gritty and the sun black, casting its great gloom over the city, and depositing drifts of ash on every windowsill, before collapsing upon itself in a smoking pile, where it smoulders still. Even in our finest moments, and in spite of our invincible desire to believe, we knew all along it had been built to burn; ever since the first Dutch wall, and the first dollar bill pasted over the counter of the first inn, we knew this island was so much kindling, a mountain of money soaked in gasoline.

AMBERGRIS

1

THERE WAS THE ANNOUNCEMENT AGAIN, THE ONE FOR THE LOST child. Or the found one, who had lost its parents—the one whose parents were lost: it depended, he supposed, on how you looked at it. They had lost each other, anyway. The child, the announcement said, was being held at the Eighty-First Street exit, like a parcel to be recovered.

It was a huge building, this much was true. But it was impossible, he thought, to truly get lost here. Everything was ordered, every alcove labeled and mapped, all the chapels and wayward passages locked, or under supervision. The most you could hope for was to be misplaced, to be, somehow, out of order.

2

For most of the day the museum is overrun by children. Left largely to themselves, they move in packs, like feral dogs. There are so many children that the adults present actually seem larger.

Hardly surprising, then, that one occasionally goes missing. Perhaps this allows the museum to function normally the remainder of the time—even ensures the safety of all the other children.

As closing time nears, the running, shrieking hordes begin to retreat, exposing many of the museum's most dazzling gems to the opportunity for silent appreciation. The fossil halls on the top floor are among the last to empty. But it is possible that, at the very end of the day, like the last vertebra in a sauropod's tail, like the few seconds of human history measured on the clock of geological time, he will have a moment to himself. The moment is enough. It grows into something much greater than the time it ostensibly occupies, in just the way the strong, slant light of the low-hanging sun at that hour elongates—some would say distorts—the shadows of the objects it touches: the southeast turret of the museum, the statue of Teddy Roosevelt on his horse, the trees along the avenue, the people milling around food carts and subway entrances. Staring out of the tall windows, he might even see himself emerge from the park, then fidget on the corner until his father catches up with him and takes his hand, to cross the avenue together.

He will sit in the turret like a captive princess, genuflecting discreetly, until a guard comes and ferrets him out. He will not even remember hearing the closing announcement.

3

The car-sized hunk of stone in the middle of the Hall of the Universe, a fragment recovered from the Willamette meteorite, is the warm bronze color of the T. rex skull in the Hall of Saurischian Dinosaurs, though many times heavier. It is made of iron, like the head of an ancient weapon. A slow-trickling acid has eaten holes in it, giving it a kind of face, or at least an expression, possibly of contrition.

Where impact by objects falling from space is concerned, extinction and kinetic energy are closely correlated: the greater the mass, and the higher the velocity—the latter squared—the more widespread the disaster. A meteorite the size of the museum, for example, would do considerable damage, that is, on the scale of a city: millions dead, though this only in the unlikely event that it were to strike an urban center, so much of the earth being only marginally habitable, and such a great percentage covered by water. A meteorite the size of Manhattan, however, is another story. Such meteorites appear with relative infrequency. As a general rule, frequency and object size are directly proportional, so that, for every increase in the size of an object by five or so times, its frequency decreases by an order of magnitude. Thus, a meteorite the size of Central Park, or about as wide across as the path he and his father would walk every Sunday to the museum, only falls every few million years, or about ten for every Manhattan-size meteor. A meteorite the size of the museum, on the other hand, falls with messiah-like frequency. Smaller ones—the size of a subcompact car or large household appliance—generally burst apart in the stratosphere, showering the earth with debris. Such impacts are usually more comic than tragic: a hole in the roof of the family station wagon, say.

These general rules should be relatively comforting for the species of the earth, including his. But he finds little solace in this sort of interstellar gambling. The museum tells him that scientists have mapped more than 90 percent of Manhattan-sized (i.e., catastroph-ic) meteorites. This is a bright way of saying that almost 10 percent remain unaccounted for. If ten tigers were to be released randomly in the museum, one would hardly be comforted by the news that nine of them had been captured. And this figure did not account for the far larger number of Central Park-sized meteorites capable of inflicting destruction on a continental scale. These are much more difficult to trace. Even assuming that the 90 percent figure reduced the frequency by a factor of ten, without knowing when the last such meteor had struck (was it at the end of the Cretaceous, or the end of the Permian? The end of something, certainly), the world might be overdue. As the museum portends:

"The question of future catastrophic impacts is not if, but when."

So-called wild card comets paint an even bleaker picture. "Even a relatively small comet," the museum says, "would impact the earth with extremely high energy"—the square of the velocity being the cul-prit here—"and little warning. Trillions of comets"—trillions!—"are hidden"—hidden!—"in a zone far beyond Pluto's orbit called the Oort cloud."

After a catastrophic impact, the fossil record shows a clear before and after. A whole new evolutionary act has begun, separated from the previous by an iridium scrim. Such an event erases an entire his-tory of life, burying it in the mass grave of its crater, and in the mol-ten and gaseous rock thrown into the air, and so on, through all the subsidiary cataclysms: earthquakes, tidal waves, burning winds. If any life manages to escape these horrors, it will more than likely suffocate, starve, or freeze to death under a world-blanketing cloud of dust.

Yet, it is never—has never been—total. Something always per-sists; something always crosses that capillary in the rock. But there is no going back, and no memory of what happened before, beyond a few dead fragments that can no longer be assembled into a story.

4

He was supposed to run an errand but got sidetracked in the museum, the museum to whose labyrinthine corridors his father used to bring him every week after church. He was supposed to pick up flour, or maybe it was sugar—it might have been milk—something, anyway, for the life of him he couldn't remember what. None of these things sounded plausible; they were too generic, too much the sorts of things anyone would be charged to stop for, and so were likely just placeholders for the thing itself. Except that the things he used to fill that hole (sugar, milk, flour, one after another, like notches in a turning wheel) in no way signified anything about the purpose of the errand, and so could not really serve as a mnemonic, except for the idea that there was something to remember. And what did knowing there was something to remember help, when the specific thing he was supposed to remember was irretrievably lost? And then he became suspicious that the placeholders themselves (milk, flour, sugar) were actually responsible for his amnesia: that they had infiltrated and devoured the original content, like a bird devouring another's eggs and commandeering its nest. Their purpose was not actually to help him remember but to cause him to forget, and the only thing that was beyond their power to eradicate was that there was something to be forgotten.

5

"The moon," the museum says, "was probably formed in the wake of a titanic collision between the earth and a smaller planet." He has read these words dozens of times, studied the drawing of the moon's birth. But the magnitude of the catastrophe—a million Manhattans pummeling the earth all at once—still escapes him, as does the idea that anything could be born from it, even if it was just a dead gray thing, hovering in space, offering only reflected light.

The comet that struck Jupiter in 1997 caused earth-sized devastation there. Which is to say that, had it struck the earth instead, nothing would have survived. No birds, no scrawny little cave mammals, no ammonites. Nothing.

Did Earth have any recollection of the time before the cataclysm, when it was pregnant with the moon?

It wasn't birth. It was more like the amputation caused by an explosion. A photo he had once seen from the war in Vietnam: a human leg, lying in the middle of a Vietnamese street. Someone was pedaling by on a bike when the picture was snapped.

6

He was born just days after Armstrong said the famous words: he was that small step and that giant leap. Boundless, going places. His mother liked to say he wouldn't have been born if the astronauts had missed the moon, and sometimes he imagined himself drifting between womb and world. His parents had even made up a fake birth certificate with his name and coordinates—somewhere on the Descartes Highlands—which he taped to his wall beside the photograph of Armstrong's gray boot print and the facsimile of his signature. It was as miraculous as the fossilized tracks left by australopithecines in the African savannah three million years ago.

The big couch in the middle of the room where his mother sat was the sun. Holding him over his head, his father would slingshot them around the couch, zooming past the TV (Earth) and telephone (moon), fly by the planets of the outer solar system (his mother asked them not to move the furniture, so relative distances were hardly representative) and on to the nearest stars (e.g., toilet, tub: Alpha Centauri A, B).

He had a good memory for the names of the constellations and craters and lunar seas, just as he did for dinosaurs, and birds, and even for the saints that the church preserved in aspic. But the last Apollo mission had flown before he'd made his first memory. It was as alien to him as his own birth. They had simply put the moon away, like you might a toy you were no longer interested in. It had a charge, but no memory; it crackled, like a broken message through an intercom. A toy, stored in the attic of the sky, which creaked opened every day at dusk.

7

Coming as late in the day as he did, he sometimes felt like the museum was perpetually in the act of closing. He blushed to think of some of the ploys he'd used to extend his time by a few minutes. Choose the points farthest from any exit. Avoid the approaching guard without appearing to do so. Pretend not to see them until a second guard intervened, or a wall. Then, when they had him cornered, pull out his planner and pretend to jot down notes, scribbling away faster when they warned him in a test-proctor's voice that his time was up, but never look their way, never, until they came at him as a group, like orderlies in an asylum. *Then* he would start walking, but slowly, so slowly he could barely keep his balance, less bipedal, more two-wheeled, trying to pedal at a crawl, and so reeling through one hall after another, as if to make the absolute longest distance between two points yet longer. Some days he affected a limp; he had feigned deafness, pretended not to speak English—it *was* embarrassing, this impish, juvenile rebellion, but then he always did feel a bit like a boy again when he came here. It was *why* he came here, and it was only partly manifested in the quiet wonder with which he regarded the museum itself. Besides, he was positive they purposefully set their watches a little ahead in order to rob him of precious moments. They must have recognized him—God knows he recognized them—coming always on the same day of the week, at the same time, playing some version of the same mischief. Probably they had his picture up somewhere, like a shoplifter's.

Their strategies of capture and his of avoidance would have evolved in tandem. He had, for example, contemplated hiding inside one of the exhibits. In fact, one day he had ducked inside the diorama of the sperm whale and giant squid, the only diorama in the whole museum without a glass shield. It was one of his most vivid memories, though he must have been very young when it happened, and he could never be entirely certain it actually *had* happened, that he hadn't dreamt the whole thing. It had taken all his courage, he remembered, to climb into that dark hole—hidden under the staircase that led to the balcony, in the rear corner of the lower level of the Hall of Ocean Life—to climb into the darkness where he had never even dared thrust his arm, always certain that the air felt colder even at the rim, as the water at that depth would. Climbing inside had felt like climbing over the edge of a precipice. He had worked his way around the whale's jaw, and the whale's snout, into the blackness behind. He had no recollection of why he had decided to climb inside, or what had followed.

8

It would have happened this way: the child took off running toward some exhibit it was anxious to see, while the parents, or parent—likely just one, the less assertive of the two, the one the child could walk all over—called after. When the child had slipped off—around a corner, or into a thicket of patrons, the museum was always crowded, so crowded—he broke into a half jog, pausing at the point where the child was last seen. There was no reason to be alarmed, not yet, not until it was really clear the child was gone, vanished, poof—then the panic would come out in his voice, cracking like a faulty intercom when he called the child's name. He would accost every remotely similar child he happened upon—a little too roughly, judging from their parents' reactions, though understandable, given the circumstance—and one security guard after another, until they formed an ad hoc search party. He thought not about the child but about what he would tell his spouse, and how happily he would swallow his embarrassment about overreacting if the child were to appear, as the guards assured him over and over it would, yes, it's a big place, but no one can really get lost here.

9

A floor plan of the museum is distributed to visitors with their tickets. Because no ticket is required to enter the museum after five, he never receives a floor plan. He has always prided himself on knowing his way around the museum without it.

One day, however, he noticed that the cover of the floor plan featured a detail from Charles Knight's painting of a mosasaur, which hangs under the tail of the mosasaur fossil in the Hall of Vertebrate Origins, among suspended wing bones and fish jaws whose steady, slow rocking you can only detect from their shadows. By and large he didn't care for artists' conceptions of extinct animals. They were perfect as they were, as skeletons. But Knight, whose paintings had graced the fossil halls since his childhood, was an exception.

Once he had oriented himself—it took him a moment to adjust his perception to the bird's-eye schematic—what drew his attention was how much of the museum he didn't know. Whole wings were painted red, signifying Human and Culture Halls, which he could not remember ever having visited. According to the plan, the Hall of Northwest Coast Indians could serve as a shortcut between North American Mammals and Meteorites. But he was certain he'd never walked through it.

It occurred to him then that the only reason he didn't need a map was because he never stepped off the narrow path he'd worn since his childhood, when he began coming here with his father on those Sundays after church.

Even more disturbing was the proportion of the floor plan not assigned any color but a light gray. Some of these areas were labeled as theaters and labs and libraries, clearly off-limits to patrons. Others were explicable architecturally; the Hall of Ocean Life, for example, spans three stories, the rib-vaulted ceiling stretching to the second floor, the floor sunken to the lower level, like a cellar in the sea, to make room for the blue whale to hang. But there were many, many other areas on the plan that could not be accounted for.

Places the guards hid during the day, he thought, to emerge all at once at closing.

Places children got lost, disappeared, never to be heard from again.

Except . . .

10

When he was little, the horses in the hall of advanced Mammals had all faced in the direction of time's arrow, growing larger as you moved from right to left, like elephants on parade. According to the museum, "This made evolution seem like a single straight-line projection from the earliest known horse, *Hyacotherium*, to *Equus*, the horse we know today. We now know, however, that horse evolution has been more like a branching bush than a tree with a single main trunk." To-day, the old horses are surrounded by many more recently discovered ones, facing backward as well as forward. Some even stand at odd angles to time; they make alcoves and cul-de-sacs, shrink as often as they grow. The new horses seem to be speaking with the older ones from their different vantage points in time. Leaning close, he sometimes imagines he can hear the hum of their conversation.

It is not the museum of his childhood, the place he spent all of Mass thinking about instead of God, the only thing that held him still and quiet, the cool, dusty, murmuring echo of the names of beasts spoken end to end: *Triceratops horridus, Styracosaurus albertensis, Monoclonius crassus*, amen. Even the places he knows—or thought he knew—are different. Different, and yet the same. Like him. He never stopped coming. In a way, he never left. They grew up together; and so, like a friend or sibling, even as the museum changed, its history punctuated by the renovations of many of the halls he still visited, it remained essentially the same. This continuity became a mirror and guarantor of his own. All he had to do was stay in the company of these bones and rocks and plants and animals that never aged, in this place where all of time was constellated around him.

If one says that one is not the same person one was twenty years before, what exactly does this mean? When did the change occur? If it didn't happen all at once, like a meteorite strike, but gradually, cumulatively, then couldn't one assert this about every successive moment in time? Was he as different as, say, a son from his father? As one species from its nearest relative on the tree of life? As the animatronic, computerized museum of today from the old, dusty place where his mother refused to set foot, where the horses all faced the same direction and grew progressively larger?

A renovation, he thinks, is nothing like a meteorite strike. The past—his, the museum's—is carefully preserved, like the horses of his childhood, shining like beacons through the vacuum of the intervening years, framed inside a more complex story. What he fears is the spaces between the branches, between the old museum and the new one as it folds back upon itself, between the terminal buds on the cladogram.

11

In some of the pictures that hang along the corridor leading to the Eighty-First Street exit, the moon looks like a bone; in others, a blastocyst; in others, a tumor. A faceless face looming out of the darkness. Craters like pores. Ridges like veins. The moon has a hidden face, the boundary between it and its nearside marked by shadow. The moon has no atmosphere; "the sun," the museum says, "shines more brightly in the vacuum." The moon has the preternatural clarity of tiny creatures viewed under a scanning electron microscope. Seen from the void of space, distance and size become difficult to judge. The earth rolls up over the moon's horizon like the sun does over the earth's. It is possible to slip off the surface of the moon and into the surrounding nothingness. Craters like pores, ridges like veins. The moon has a hidden face. Not just distance and size, time is all a garble. As though time had a gravity that can be escaped, satellites with which it was associated, so that, falling into the voids between, one lists in a direction that is no direction, neither backward nor forward, searching for some reference point to set time aright, to get it flowing in a direction, any direction. Time a puddle not a stream.

Nothing had ever been more directed, more carefully planned, than the Apollo missions. And yet, there had never been anything in the history of the world further off the beaten path. Not even Columbus, daring the edge of the world. A real loop through the void, a cosmic hernia that, for all the precise calculation it took to bring off, must have felt unmeasurable to the astronauts—and even to mission control, in the bare, crackling contact through space. They must have felt it, perhaps not at the beginning of the mission, but toward the end: a sensation of immortality, but stripped of power. Instead, terror: of having fallen off the world, of being a speck lost in the cosmos, transferred to the cosmos of time. Yes, they had helmets and space-suits, rocket engines and re-entry shields, radios and monitors linking them to an ever-vigilant mission control, locking their coordinates moment by moment. But what protection could there be against such a feeling?

12

He should have been one of many patrons driven toward the exits like buffalo over a cliff. He was always bringing up the rear, it was true, but with the line of guards behind him (and more always appearing), it was impossible to dawdle.

The museum was already closed. There was no other explanation for the emptiness, the overwhelming silence in which his footfalls echoed, never audible in the daytime.

He had heard the preliminary announcements: half an hour, ten minutes. He just could not remember how long ago. Something always happened to time here. Where disparate geographies were thrust side by side, and one could traverse millions of years and orders of magnitude in a few steps—in such a jumble of scales and sizes, distances and years, how could time help but lose its harder edges? How could he ever hope to get anywhere if he kept shrinking and growing tenfold, jumping back and forth over millions of years while seas and continents collided and disappeared around him?

But the closing announcement—had he heard it at all? Had he simply been distracted? Missed the guards, or they him? Deliberately, in retribution for all the games he'd played around closing?

And now here he was, on the other side of that moment. Lost.

Not lost. The screens might all go blank, the voices and ambient noises slur to a halt, the whole museum power down to silence and darkness, drift like an abandoned ocean liner, but he would still not be lost.

How long he had wished to have the museum all to himself. The quiet, the emptiness. Not a living soul. Just him.

And the child, he reminded himself. The one that was lost, abandoned maybe. Forgotten.

The noise of footfalls, not his own. He paused, just to be certain, heard and felt his heart, two for every step, almost. A mouse's beats six hundred times a minute. An elephant's. A whale's.

If he was found, he would pretend that he was lost, and the guard would escort him to the nearest exit. And then everything would feel real, excruciatingly real, as though the world had emerged from a cocoon.

Avoid the guards, then. Avoid them at any cost.

13

He should be more patient, he thinks, with children. More tolerant. His father, after all, rarely lost his temper with him. His father, who used violence reluctantly, and only at his mother's urging. His mother, though. Her size belied her strength, and she grabbed whatever was nearest at hand. It was an incentive to put things away.

"Grow up!" she would shout. "Both of you!"

God, if she had seen him and his father on those Sunday afternoons. Only the joggers outpaced them, bright shorts and long socks rushing toward the green battlements of the park's east side like bees toward a hive. He took his father's hand at the intersections, in the park not at all. In the tunnels they whistled and hollered and stamped their feet until they were deaf from the echo. On the mall they swooped around the easels and parasols, around the instrument cases glistening with coins, making noises with their mouths like spitfires.

Sometimes, after church, when his mother was helping him put on his sneakers, she would say, out of the corner of her mouth, "Take care of your dad. Don't let him out of your sight." Like he was taking his father to the museum, not the reverse. And his father would turn out his bottom lip, pretend to mope, like the statue of Beethoven on the mall. Except that he was more like the manatee in the Hall of Ocean Life.

Sometimes he fantasizes about the museum implementing a schedule like a swimming pool. For fifteen minutes of every hour, the children would have to line up along the perimeters of the halls in absolute silence, giving the adults an opportunity to observe the exhibits unimpeded. Or a whole day every week might be set aside. Or the museum might stay open later on certain evenings.

If only patrons were made to check their children at the bag counter. Except after five, when the bag counter was closed. It was the reason he was allowed to keep his, always.

It was no use, of course. The fault lay with the parents. They were the ones who abandoned their children to the museum. Open the museum up to them, and they would act worse than their kids.

Then again, these were also the adults who would never forget whatever petty errand they had been charged with.

Flour. Milk. Sugar.

The museum had meant something different then, when he was a boy, what seemed like a million years ago, before severed legs could lie unattended in the street while people biked by. The sum of human

93

knowledge, towering like Everest; the museum, an ark afloat on the waters of time, carrying that knowledge into the future and beyond the edges of the solar system. The faith had been deep and wide-spread, the cargo and mission sacred.

And so, yes, he should be more patient with children. Try to guide them, even if counteracting years of neglect is like trying to squeeze blood from a stone. Sidle up to them, smile at them, wait for them to smile back or stare at you wide-eyed, as though you were the object of wonder. Tell them something startling about whatever they happened to be looking at. Such as: "A meteorite that size would kill everyone on the earth ten times over." Or: "That whale can dive a mile deep and hold its breath for hours." It did no good scowling, or knocking them down, as he had done on a few occasions. Passively, of course: the child come running, distracted. A collision fated by phys-ics. Orbits unalterable. Nobody's fault. Anyway, children are resilient. Practically indestructible. Not like adults. Within a few minutes they would have completely forgotten it had happened. Or not complete-ly. It would be there, somewhere. They might be more careful next time, running; they just would not know why.

14

They used to come here every Sunday, he and his father—his mother had no interest, she said, in "those old, dusty things." (His father said there was nothing older and dustier than her "goddamn church.") Always to see the same old, dusty things, in the same order:

The recovered fragment of the Willamette meteorite.

The moon, as it had appeared to the astronauts on the last Apollo voyage.

The earth, with and without its oceans.

The horse and its extinct relatives.

Mammals, African or North American (various).

Whales: blue and sperm.

There were dozens of other exhibits he acknowledged in passing, genuflecting as necessary: T. rex (skull), woolly mammoth and mastodon, mosasaur, moschops, oarfish, giant clam, etc. But there were only a few where he was bound to pay his respects. The proper amount of time had to be spent with each, only he could say how long. That was the best part about coming. At the museum, time was his. As he finished at each station, he would turn to look at his father, and his father, if he was not too distracted with the paper or some pretty girl's stocking or some piece of foreign matter between his teeth, would say, "Ready?" But he was already walking—never running, like the other children. He didn't need Father Esposito, or Mrs. Ruane, or any adult, to tell him *that*. Not even his father, trailing somewhere far behind.

He spent the biggest portion of the afternoon among the dioramas of mammals. At first he had leaned over the wooden rails, his nose so near that it almost touched the glass, and sometimes did, *whap*, always a shock, no matter how light the tap. Not that he was dozing, though his trancelike devotion may have appeared that way to an onlooker; not like his father, seated on a bench nearby, one foot kicked forward with the toe of his shoe up. His father had given up trying to read the paper in the dim light of some savannah or mountain scene, folded it up on the bench beside him and, hands palm-up in his lap, fingers laced, had fallen asleep, his light snore lost in the murmur: the manatee, asleep above the sea grass.

He took two steps back and paused, framed in the lighted glass of the diorama, like a projection of his father's dream.

15

For a time they had pretended it didn't mean anything, wasn't a harbinger. They had both felt it, the first trickles of that acid eating away at their hearts. Some months later, when the medical verdict had come back, they claimed not to understand it, and then refused to believe it. The child looked normal, healthy; what did it matter if it was a little unresponsive? It had been a little premature, a little small; it was shy, that was all. They had gotten through that time together, when it was monitored like a tiny astronaut inside a capsule. The child was fine; everyone had said so. The rest was prognostication, like the weather. Nobody had a crystal ball. They said these things to each other, and to themselves, while the trickle grew.

It did not develop like other children, that was true. More slowly. Then not at all. There was a difference of opinion about where it might get to, but there was no question that it was not where it *should be* for its age, or that the gap between was and should be would continue to grow. The years moved more slowly for it, he said; the apex of its development was reserved for some time in the distant future. It would live for ages, like a sequoia tree, and this longevity would compensate for everything.

This worked for a time, or would have, had they been able to freeze it before they really knew (they always knew), before they suspected (they always suspected), when it was still natural, or at least plausible, that the child could do nothing for itself, that it would cry every moment it was awake. For all its inability to do anything, it was quite adept at injuring itself. It even managed to injure them. Strong for its size, though the spasmodic nature of its movements had to be taken into consideration. After it blackened her eye, they restrained it, as they had been advised to do from the first.

The priest could offer no more consolation than the doctors. He was clearly uncomfortable with its wailing, could barely make himself heard. His words kept coming back, the ones about the bright future, heralded by the child's miraculous preservation. But they had watched helplessly as the miracle child folded up, twisted back upon itself, like an animal whose ligaments have dried.

She would recite litanies each night, staring at the ceiling, of all the things it would never do. That was the reality, the reality she claimed he refused to face. And he never stopped her when she took out her feelings of having been wronged on the child. How could he, when he felt the same way? He could not even bring himself to say anything. But neither would he permit himself to leave the room. "Too stupid even to smile back at you," she'd say. "Even a fucking dog can smile back at you. *What is wrong with you?*" What is wrong with you?

He could no longer remember its name, Latinate or common, or whether it was boy or girl. Could not have said what it looked like, except for its deformity. There were pictures—buried somewhere so they would not have to be looked at—that reminded them of the obvious, of how clear it had been from the start.

16

The spinning half globe affixed to the ceiling of the hall of Planet Earth leaches out the clouds, the seas, until the earth, cloudless and dry, looks like a brown moon. Then it fills back up again, beginning with the deepest trenches, the abyssal plains. It is a miracle, he thinks, that the water doesn't keep rising and rising until the whole planet is blue, and whales could swim over the peak of Everest.

He likes to hold his breath while the ocean basins fill, exhale as they leach out. The whole cycle has a rhythm, like breathing.

"The earth," the museum says, "never sleeps." He has never been sure how they can tell.

"Life," the museum says, "may have begun around deep hydrothermal vents. If similar environments exist elsewhere in the solar system, they too may support life." But then the earth, it tilts and wobbles, its orbit becomes more or less eccentric, and these changes, seemingly so innocent, turn the world from fire to ice, and back again, cyclically. Plotted against time, everything is a wave, and life, or most of it, has ended and begun over and over again, as naturally as breathing, or a wave lapping shore, tugged by the limb that hovers like a ghost on the horizon, offering only reflected light, and reminding the earth of its once having been complete.

17

One day he stepped off the main path in the hall of advanced Mammals and ended up on the wrong side of the horses. The writing was inverted, as in a mirror, and the bones faced left to right. Who knows how old he was, or where his father was. His father might already have been dead.

From this angle, one can view not only the horses, but the museum's other patrons as well, the ones who did not take the fork. They too seem to be on display, and they shuffle past wearing expressions of mute alarm, like carousel horses. They seem to be going in the wrong direction, and too quickly, slipping over the horizon of time like water down a cataract, each patron a drop, together a mighty roar. Watching them, he felt like one of the horses behind the glass, the patrons in their own time, a separate current he could never hope to rejoin, an adjacent branch on the evolutionary tree. As he reached out to touch the nearest horse's flank, his hand struck the glass, and the museum roar rushed back to his ears, loud as a cataract.

One day, a child hid inside the whale, the sperm whale, entered it like some still-defiant Jonah, like a willing sacrifice, climbed around the whale's narrow jaw and great blunt snout, crawling into the deepest deep and the darkest dark, to a place where no one would ever think to look, dream or dare to go, a place that was indeed outside the jurisdiction of God, or their God, because they would never think to rub the whale's snout like a horse's, because they would never smile to it until it promised to smile back, because they felt neither reverence for it nor kinship with it.

18

The child was dead. only the echo of its voice remained, audible when the daytime murmur ceased and the recorded sound effects were turned off, preserved in these chambers like the sea inside a conch, like the hum of an insect trapped inside a glass. The announcement was a recording, set to play throughout the day, every X minutes, like the one accompanying the spinning half globe.

Or: There never was a child, just the idea of one. The desire for one. It was a trap; he was the insect. A false trail, toward an objective that did not exist, to get him lost.

Except that nothing . . .

He paused, shifted his backpack, felt the weight inside it shift, heavy enough to be flour. Or sugar. Or . . .

Perhaps, he thought, he was not supposed to pick something up but leave something. The fact that he could not remember what it was didn't matter. Couriers weren't paid to know what they were delivering. Sometimes it was in their best interest not to know.

19

He brought the child to the museum every week, as he had always intended to, but with a new objective. He had the ridiculous idea (even he admitted it) that exposing the child to all the wonders of nature, presented so compellingly as they were in the museum, would manage to jump-start its intellect. It was, after all, the great unsolved mystery of human evolution: what had happened, what had been the discovery, the encounter, the environmental shift that had caused our brains to begin expanding? He would solve the problem by folding time back on itself: the ape-man, the early hominid, confronts its own image in the abandoned museum; this glimpse of its future creates a retroactive self-consciousness. And so he carried, and pointed, and talked incessantly, in answer to every unasked question he could think of, reading placards aloud, shouting sometimes; and the child hollered, and drooled, and swung its head about in every direction but the exhibit they were supposed to be looking at, and fell again to the floor, writhing. Sometimes it seemed to him not only not his child, but a creature of a totally different species, genus, family. Rate of mutation: distance in time. He stopped caring that other people were watching, whether pitying him or annoyed by the noise. They were alone together in their capsule, just as he had imagined them in those touch-and-go weeks at the very beginning.

Then it picked itself up and started away, dragging its feet sideways, almost walking on all fours. Dinosaurs had become birds, apes men, men astronauts. There was no limit to what was possible.

20

One day he looked around him and found that he recognized nothing. A feeling like waking in an unfamiliar room, head lying in the wrong direction, door and windows exchanged. It was the museum of colors he had never visited, wormholes between the halls he knew; of unaccounted-for grays, folds in the map; of gaps in the cobblestone flow of time. He remembered walking up the stairs, worn into saddles by a century's rain of shoes. That had been eons ago. Even the most recent moments stretched away from him, like planets from the sun.

But then it was a long time since he had been able to remember the recent past with any clarity. The museum had shrunk it to a mote in the vista of deep time.

If, through a process of successive analogies, the idea of magnitude, for example, became grounded in the scale of human experience, the reverse was also true: the human threatened to dissolve in ideas of the infinitesimally small and infinitely large, immeasurable distances and remote ages.

Evolution was a thicket, a swamp, earth unredeemed by spade or plow. No more single straight path anywhere. No more the feeling that everything was being propelled toward some great impending future that pulled with a fate like gravity. Only the meteorite, aimless, contrite, hurtling toward them, to birth unforeseeable new worlds from the crater.

He must have slipped orbits somewhere, derailed. And if he had indeed fallen outside the rut that had made a museum of his life, perhaps he'd see himself, run into himself, as he had been. A foreign body, hurtling toward a familiar orbit, impact pending. What dead thing would their collision bring to light?

He saw himself rushing ahead of his father, but when he looked behind him, no one was there.

If he kept looking ahead, if he walked far enough, if he let time come up to his neck and then over his head, if he could follow the loop he mistook for a line because it was too wide to reckon the curve, then maybe, maybe he would find the horses all facing in the same direction again, and growing.

21

Floating above, the whale was nothing but a belly, huge and grooved. When sometime later he stood and headed to the back corner of the hall, under the back staircase, leaving his father asleep, he felt light as krill.

He could see the squid before the whale—the squid, never seen alive in its natural habitat, the grainy edge of human knowledge. The whale was just beyond it, half-embraced by it, and impossible to see until his eyes adjusted. Slowly it resolved: the top of the head, spotted by the shadow of the squid's unattached tentacles; the silhouette of the narrow jaw; the snout, the eye. The absence of light, of background, of glass to isolate the space from his; the fact that only the head of the whale was visible, as if it had floated up silently beside the hole—all of it conspired to create the feeling of immense depth. It was as though, crossing the hall, the floor dropped like a mine shaft, every step spanned fathoms—were he to slip, he would fall in to the hole at the bottom of the museum; or as though the whole hall were a bathysphere, and the only thing that was keeping the whale out was some trick of pressure. Looking up, he saw that the blue whale had shrunk to the size of a passing jet. He could no longer see his father at all. He hung on to the edge of the diorama. Let go with one hand, reached in—cold, so much colder in there, beyond where the glass should be. Let go with the other. And then he was floating, falling, tumbling into the darkness beyond the whale's snout.

22

One day he was watching it stumble away, pitching its head from side to side and lowing, when a strange feeling of detachment came over him, as though the child were not his at all but an exhibit that had come to life, hurdled the railing around it, or broken the glass keeping it in, and was in the process of escaping from the museum. The idea held him transfixed for a time, long enough for the child to disappear into the oncoming crowds. It was audible for a short time after, lowing. When he finally started after it, he could not bring himself to run more than halfheartedly, certainly not panic, since nothing could be more obvious than the child, his, stumbling through the halls, hollering and drooling. Nor could he bring himself to report the missing child (who was not really missing, not yet) to a guard. All these delays and evasions. It was impossible for the child to get lost; someone would see it, notice it, hold it. (Have their eye blackened. Why would they touch the damn thing?) Walking quickly (never running, not in the museum) from hall to hall, he recalled the moment without it, alone. He had not even heard the crowds. It was his father's fault, clearly. Distracted, asleep, he was the reason the child got too far ahead, fell outside of radio contact, the gulf between them filling with ocean, with the brightness of the vacuum. He would tell her about it, later, after she had exhausted herself yelling, like he was the child. She blamed him, he knew, because he had done, finally, passively, what she could not bring herself to, what the daily abuse ensured she never could, and what she was really saying by yelling at him was thank you.

23

The museum will be closing in half an hour, in ten minutes, in nineteen seconds, before the Spanish rendering of this announcement is complete. Please make your way to the nearest exit. The museum is now closed. The museum has been closed for some time now; what are you still doing here? The guards are coming in their buffalo hides, caning the glass windows of the dioramas, emerging from under the benches and behind the columns and out of the secret doors. Fly, little bird. Hide. Hide, before they force you out, back into the night, into the noise and chaos of the city, the dreadful exposure, crawling around the traffic, the horns and the swerving automobiles, the pummeling shoes and rain, the searching lights. A broken siren, a gnawing sound, a pungent odor, strong as perfume. No refuge, no way back. We hope you have enjoyed your visit.

24

The most important thing was to stay absolutely still. For longer than seemed humanly possible. Everything hinged on this.

For most children his age, this was difficult; for him, simply unthinkable. Sparrow, his mother called him, chided him. But what kind? There were a number of different species of sparrow on display in the diorama of common northeastern birds in Roosevelt Memorial Hall. He liked the vesper sparrow best, because of the way it sounded.

For a long time he had not understood the importance of immobility. He would pace like a fighter goading his opponent in front of the glass, and then freeze suddenly, as if to surprise time and the apparent solidity of things. The idea of mimicking the animals, which, to better project the illusion of life, were posed in some representative behavior—the great horned owl carrying a meal to her young; the grizzly cub shimmying up a spruce trunk; the blue-lit wolves suspended in motionless chase—that much made sense. But he had underestimated the time it would take.

From this failed strategy of freezing in different places, he discovered that each diorama had a single ideal point from which it should be seen. The rear wall on which the surrounding landscape was painted curved around an implicit focus, like space curving around a center of gravity. To find it, he needed to step back a little—pressing his face up to the glass just distorted the scene, like fish swimming along the window of an aquarium—though never so far that the diorama's frame or title would impinge too distinctly on the corners of his vision, or that some patron might feel invited to cross in front.

It also mattered where he focused his attention. Over time, he discovered that the edge where the stage (on which the sculpted rocks and trees and taxidermied animals were mounted) met the curving wall and ceiling (on which landscape and sky were painted to create the illusion of space and distance) was often artfully hidden with tall grass or a cliff's edge. If he fixed his vision on that inferred edge for long enough, and then longer still—and all this supposing he had discovered the correct viewpoint—then at some point the planes would merge: the distance was no longer an illusion, or the illusion was complete. The diorama suddenly turned into a window, as though the space represented—the shore of Gunflint Lake, Minnesota; the plains of the Great Rift Valley—had been drawn up against the museum, the way landscapes are joined in a dream.

And then one day, before the diorama of the great horned owl, he forgot everything: the placard explaining what it was he was looking at, with numbered outlines to identify flora and fauna; the opaque walls separating one diorama from the next, and the glass orifices of the adjacent windows, bathing the dim hall in light; the hard, even floor of the museum on which he had, until a moment before, stood.

The glass had dissolved, and he had passed through, just as easily as his shadow once had, when he had leaned close.

His father was on the other side. He could tell because he could see the outline of his reflection in the glass, and because the tree with the owl's nest appeared peripherally between them. The silence and stasis here were absolute. Not a leaf stirred. Even the water, though rippling, was still. And so long as he did not move, he was, like the owls, unable to age: miraculously preserved, and seemingly neither alive nor dead. He had the feeling, somewhere between a memory and a dream, that his father was behind this; that he had built the whole frozen world around him. In a few moments he would rise, pick up his paper, and shuffle slowly toward an exit, a guard pursuing him the whole way. He would be back again next week; he never missed a Sunday. But here, on this side of the glass, time moved much more slowly. Every moment was a mountain to be eroded away. He could have joined him, but that would have meant moving, and he was not yet ready to leave.

25

One day he tried to leave the museum via the eighty-first street exit and ran into this sign: Ticket Holders Only Beyond This Point.

But tickets were not required after five. The guards wouldn't even look at him; he might have been invisible.

It didn't matter that some guard had swiveled the sign around at five, to let the latecomers through, or the absurdity of the injunction itself.

How many hours had he stolen over the course of his lifetime? How many times had the museum suffered him to take advantage of a few minutes at the end of the day?

To be demanded a ticket for egress! That was poetic justice.

At the invisible border demarcated by the sign, he leaned over as far as he could and flailed his arms, hoping to catch a guard's eye. The foyer was deserted. Beyond, he could just make out the corner of the world, green and muted behind the glass.

26

He finds the empty case he has been looking for, kneels down on the white pebbles inside, and unshoulders his pack. The skeleton of the child is folded up inside like a sleeping bat. Only the skull, the most difficult part to get through, is wrapped separately. Beneath the skull is a hard plastic case with his materials and tools: pins, pliers, an awl, a dentist's drill, a small compressor. He has the whole night ahead of him, and he will work with the breathless precision of a jewel thief so that it is standing when the first patrons arrive. He, sitting on the nearest bench, pretending to sleep, will be watching.

The child must be carefully unfolded, first its crossed arms, then its legs, the knees of which are drawn up to where its chin would be. Marvelously small, even smaller than it appeared in life: a perfect miniature, a figurine. For almost a month it had been nothing but a shifting dry suit of famished beetles, which, if he leaned close to the capsule, he could hear chewing, a noise like static. At the end, with the injection of the gas, they had fallen away all at once, and the bright skeleton had lay upon their glutted corpses like a bier. It would have been more dramatic, he thought, had it been standing, and the beetles had fallen like leaves off a tree after a night's hard frost. He set about painting it then, the mythic bronze of fossilized bone.

But for the skull, no assembly is required. Most of the tools are precautionary; the work has all been done: holes drilled, pins inserted, wires cut to size. The joists have been removed for ease of transportation, and these are what he must restore, beginning with the feet. The child has done everything but stand.

In the tomb-like space of the hall, it is impossible to say how much time passes. Tedious, meticulous labor, something like wiring the lights on a Christmas tree. Now and again he licks his lips, chapped with bone dust. And he finds his mind wandering, as it always does when he is engaged in like tasks: backward, to his mother, helping him change his shoes on the steps of Saint Catherine's so that he wouldn't soil his Sunday clothes, and to the vision of the pale stone of the southeast turret as he approached it from the park, so far ahead that he could no longer hear his father's voice; forward, to the morning to come, the first patrons standing admiringly before the child.

When the skeleton is standing, complete but for the skull, it is almost as tall as his waist, and he steps back to examine his work, retreating until he finds the focus of the imaginary parabola. It stands before no painted backdrop; it is not posed so as to give the impression of being engaged in any action. It just stands: straight, complete, perfectly symmetrical. That is enough; da Vinci could do no better. In life it had never stood so erect.

Unwrapping the skull, he remembers her words: "Never put the star on the tree." It seemed like the most stupidly criminal thing about its living. He remembers the feel of the child's hair when he stroked its head, his other hand pointing at some star, or tree, or whale, some wonder, while the child stared longingly and uncomprehendingly up at him instead, as though desperate to please him. He strokes the skull absently, as he had the head, lost in thought, before stepping forward with it held up before him in both hands.

27

He had reached one of those halls where nobody ever comes. The dust his mother had abhorred was everywhere, moon-gray, coating the glass cases along the walls and the tarpaulins thrown over the dead exhibits huddled in the center of the room, revealing his own tracks across the stone floor. There was not a single window; the source of the wan light was a mystery. This, he thought, was the museum of his childhood. And yet, he had never been here before, not that he could remember. Perhaps nobody had; perhaps the hall was entirely forgotten. Perhaps he had crossed the capillary in the rock, to a point behind the moment of impact.

He walked, and as he buried himself deeper in the catacombs, they began to change around him. The even stone floor crumbled into gravel, loud under his feet. A warm, moist air settled over him. The glass disappeared, leaving the dust suspended colloidally in the air, before it too vanished. The smell of age that had chafed his nostrils upon entering was replaced by something ripe, fungal, as of newly turned earth. Figures appeared and disappeared, whether near or far it was difficult to tell, and he could hear chanting, now close, like insects in his ear, now as though across a valley. A language he was on the cusp of understanding, familiar but forgotten. For some reason, he recalled the family photo that one of the Apollo astronauts had left on the moon, in an area called the Descartes Highlands: he, wife, kids, all smiling, frozen, perfect, their color defying the gray moon dust, brought into relief by a nearby boot print, his; their lives defying the surrounding evidence of impact after impact—all life, he mused, was just such an act of idiot defiance, a race to see how much organic matter could accumulate between craters—in that place without the thinnest atmosphere for a shield. A chain of hands leading backward through time, to cave children taken by their cave fathers to see paintings of mammoths, and then further back, many times further, to the Carboniferous, the Permian, before there were hands, limbs, backbones, bones, when the whole world was water, when life was just beginning to coalesce around the warm chemical baths of deep-sea vents. Then the earth wobbled, the meteorite struck, and the chain was broken, one hand severed from the next in the long unspooling ribbon of generations. Drifting, unspooled, until the whale, that great mass, caught him in the tidal force of its gravity.

He was standing before an empty case, a white bed of pebbles, as for an exhibit that had been temporarily removed. There was no painted backdrop; the inscription on the glass was backward. He could see his shadow, and beyond it, the yet-dimmer forms of people passing like shades. They were only an arm's length away (whose arm? he wondered); the static of their conversation rippled, just audible, almost intelligible, but even so he seemed to hear them across a wide cañaveral, a sea of glass.

He thought: I have never been beyond that cañaveral. I have never stood on the opposite shore of that sea.

And then, from the other side, a voice, or the echo of one: "God, hold your nose. It smells like ambergris down here again!"

The shades vanished, the way a landscape vanishes all at once when you draw back from a window at night, and he was staring into two dark orbitals of bone, receding into craters where the eyes should have been. His feet, which had turned the fine bronze color of mineralized bone, were planted on a bed of white pebbles. It must have been a reflection in the glass he saw before; now, he was standing in just the right place.

28

Leaving the museum, he never once let go of his father's hand.

From the stadium-high vantage of Belvedere Castle, his father watched the baseball games on the Great Lawn, commenting now and again on the play. His voice sounded as distant as the crack of the bat, the applause and shouts of the players. Even holding his hand it did. He might have been encased in glass. And the same was true of the turtles, sunning themselves or paddling about in the pond far below; and, when they started walking again, of the cyclists and runners that wended past them like targets at a fair, trying to escape the winding park roads before dusk; of the horses clopping quietly by, wearing big, beautiful white feathers on their bowed heads; of the people rowing in the green glassy water of the lake, and the geese and ducks bunched on the rocks. All of it was behind glass. He was sure he could see the surface glinting between them.

By the boathouse on the east side, his father bought a pretzel and fed it to him in pieces, like he was a bird. "Swallow," he said, watching him chew absently, the white ball growing in his mouth.

It made his mother crazy, this abstraction, much more than his fidgeting did—made her "worried," made her "afraid"—and more than once she'd tried to smack it out of him, hard enough that his father winced. His father said he was just hungry. But then why did he eat so slowly, without looking at his food?

If she had seen the way he was in the park or, God forbid, the museum. But then they had been through that, had gone to see Father Esposito about it, and he had said the same thing his father had: that it was a phase. She had actually told Father Esposito it was like he was possessed when he came home, and Father Esposito had said, with a mixture of condescension and alarm, "Possessed?" Then his father had intervened, which clearly surprised everyone in the room, saying, while his hands smoothed and smoothed his slacks, that it was what the boy looked forward to all week. Then Father Esposito had spoken directly to him about the role of God in evolution, the special place of man in the universe, and a number of other things he had not really understood. Home again, putting him to bed, his mother touched his cheek and his forehead, like she was feeling for a fever. His father sighed.

"I don't let go of him," he said. "I don't let him out of my sight."

She smiled, weakly. "The blind leading the blind. It's my punishment," she said, "having a child who's just like you."

THE STABILITY OF
FLOATING BODIES

IT WAS NEVER MY INTENTION, WHEN MY FATHER CAME TO LIVE WITH us, that he would live in the pond. Things just worked out that way. This was shortly after my mother died. My wife and I had never really spoken about what we would do in the event that one of our parents died. It had always seemed a little premature to have that discussion, at least where my parents were concerned: they were in their mid-seventies, enviably lucid, and as healthy, according to their physicians, as most Americans ten years their junior. But then maybe it always seems too early. Or maybe it was that I could never imagine them apart. They had done everything together, gone everywhere together; there had been something almost tyrannical in their solicitousness about each other's welfare. One day, it occurred to me that I didn't have a single picture with just one of them in it. Were I ever to try to crop one of them out, the other would remain in the shape of the border traced by my scissors. Growing together, my mother had said to me not long before she passed, was the key to a healthy relationship; and grow together they had, like skinny trees, the trunks of which wound round each other in an act of mutual strangulation.

Even if I had been able to imagine it, I never would have expected my father to be left alone. Of the two, he was the one who needed more help. Lucid he was, but managing the phalanx of pills he had to take every day was a whole other matter. Some of them had to be broken in half, the corners sanded with a nail file to make them easier to swallow, the powder collected on a napkin and dumped into a glass of prune juice. On Sundays, after a late breakfast, my mother used to turn the kitchen table into a pharmacy counter, slicing and sorting the week's pills, and depositing the rations into each of the seven chambers of a plastic organizer the size and shape of a hockey puck. It was just one of the things my mother did for him: one of the things I would have to learn how to do.

My parents had always spoken about rest homes in the same breath as gothic torture chambers. Prisons were kindergartens by comparison. Not that the more reputable ones were within the realm of our financial possibilities, anyway. My parents had lived month to month on their social security checks and my father's tiny pension; their money all went to pay for pills, the mortgage, and the cable. Jan and I were hardly better off, what with our parochial-school salaries and the little extra we made tutoring: mortgaged up to our ears, and nearly bereft of savings. The one time I tried to help them with the little I could, my father had told me they did not accept "handouts," and insisted on treating the money as a loan. We agreed on a reasonable rate of interest. He was still paying me back when my mother died.

None of this stopped me from rattling off possibilities as I rushed around the bedroom a few hours before my flight, gathering articles of clothing, which Jan quietly folded into a suitcase. The house that had belonged to Tom Nowak's mother, for example, which he was renovating to rent out. Or the Van Duzers' house, just a half mile down the road, empty since they'd taken off for their year-long post-retirement world tour three months earlier. Or even the little barn on our property, it would require quite an influx of capital to make it livable, sure, but we had thought to do so anyway, we could manage another loan. It was temporary, I said. Temporary. Jan alternately shushed and embraced me, telling me that she would see me in a couple of days, that we would figure it out, that it would be all right. And then she gently shot down each of my ideas with the same little word, a soft bullet: stairs.

Over the last few years my father had grown progressively less steady on his feet, and whenever he talked about moving to some sunshine-state bungalow—which he had done with increasing frequency in the months before my mother died—it was always in reference to getting rid of "those damned stairs." On a flat surface devoid of obstacles, he moved well enough; but any and all stairs were like those in a funhouse, just a lever-pull away from collapsing into a slide. It was only when I was a mile up in the air, the child in the row behind me kicking my seat while he played some noisy blooping video game, and I imagining my father plummeting over and over down flights of stairs like the plane dropping out of the sky, that I was really able to parse the situation. We'd made a habit of giving our parents our bedroom whenever they visited, while we slept downstairs in the guest room, which had a futon that we kept folded into a couch and a small escritoire under the window. We called this room, half-jokingly, the meditation room, although neither of us made a habit of meditating, at least in any formal way. It was actually the one space in the house that allowed us to get away from each other. We took pains not to monopolize it; we did everything short of make a schedule. If the door was closed, we knew better than to knock. For each of us, the need for such a room seemed to come from a similar place. Jan had grown up the oldest of five siblings in a cramped little brick house in Queens; even after she started commuting to college, she did not have her own room. I was an only child, but for some reason—because there were only three of us, maybe—privacy had never been an expectation. Doors had flapped vestigially on their hinges. Later, when I moved away for college, I understood what solitude was, and how much I craved it.

I have a vivid recollection of my father coming down the stairs on the day of the funeral. We were standing in the foyer, my wife and I, we were all dressed and ready to go; and there came my father, in his dark suit, sliding from one stair to the next on his rear. He would shuffle his feet forward to the step ahead, and then ease himself down as far as he could on the heels of his hands, and then drop, thud. The chandelier would tinkle, and the framed pictures lining the stairs would tremble slightly. He was smiling as he descended, like it was a game, and for a moment I thought of him as an orphan. Even on the flight down I had been wondering if there was some way to arrange his staying here, if we could manage to afford a home health aide. I might just as well leave him in the street to die. I could feel Jan staring at me, whether anxiously or accusingly, and I knew what she was thinking: that I should run up the stairs and take him by the elbow, help him stand; with one hand in mine and the other on the banister, my arm around his waist, I could save him from this unspeakable indignity, this travesty of mourning.

Watching him, I froze.

At the viewing, empty but for Jan and me, a few of my parents' neighbors, and some relatives I had not seen in years, I did something

I had not anticipated: I touched my mother's face in the coffin. Her skin felt waxy, and my finger left a smudge. I did it once, quickly, just to know that I had done it.

Standing on our porch, my father took a deep breath, the kind that says *country air*. Though a little shrunken, he still stood straight as a new nail, not even the hint of a stoop—and this after coming down the stone path backwards, like he was rappelling, holding to the post-and-rail fence and waving me off whenever I offered to help. I was rolling his suitcase behind me. It kept flipping around on its little wheels. Like my father's feet, they were made for even floors and gentle slopes.

"Welt always loved this house," he said. "It's a pity I didn't go first. She'd have loved to live here."

I carried his suitcase to the meditation room while he stayed on the porch regally surveying the property. We had a few acres that included a moderately large pond bordered by stands of water irises on the north and south ends, and woods across that helped hide the house from the road, at least during the warmer months. It was beautiful at this time of year, with the irises and other early flowers in full bloom. But as I saw it now, it was treacherous, too, sloped and pitted, and crisscrossed by uneven stone paths, and the woods were cluttered with debris. The only exception was the narrow strip of lawn around the pond, and, I guess, the pond itself.

When I got back to the porch, Jan had brought my father a glass of water with a sprig of mint from our garden. "You should smile more," my father told her. "It's good for your complexion. Welt was always smiling," he said to me. "The woman absolutely glowed. It's why she looked twenty years younger than her age, until the day she passed."

He had said that a number of times, the bit about smiling. He said everything a number of times. It wasn't his memory; he just believed everything should be said a number of times. As for Jan, it had stopped bothering her, or so she said. But it still made me cringe.

"Life's too short not to enjoy it," he boomed, after smacking his lips. He had drained the glass in a gulp. He always boomed. Boomed and repeated things. It was impossible for the man to speak quietly. Jan and I mumbled by comparison. Maybe it was the time he'd spent in the military. Or after, when he'd worked as a door-to-door cutlery salesman, before moving into the industrial sales job from which, twenty-five years later, he would be laid off, his pension cut in half.

"We've set up the office for you," Jan said, louder than was strictly necessary. My eyes darted to her, but she was already on her way back inside.

"It's temporary," I said, though I didn't know who I was saying this to, and so precisely what "temporary" meant. "I hope it's comfortable."

"It's fine, Son. I really don't want to put you two out. That's not my intention at all. Don't you see? Welt made me promise I'd come."

He had already told us this. It was typical: anything that might show weakness was attributed to my mother. He made her out to be the coddling kind, she grew into that role for him, and by doing that she protected him from his own neediness. It was his greatest weapon, this neediness, the one thing my mother could never defend herself against. All the booming and repeating and lip-smacking were just other ways of hiding it. In a way, I envied him. I had no such brash exterior behind which I could hide. Any possibility of developing one had been weathered away by my father's voice. Nor did I have a spouse who felt compelled to shelter me.

I left him on the porch looking out on the pond, breathing his country air and swinging his strong, gnarled arms so that his hands clapped in front of him. Jan was in the kitchen, making sandwiches. These were the sorts of goodwill gestures she would perform in retreat, from isles of hard-won privacy. She knew that my parents were accustomed to eating at specific hours; when they visited, we would rearrange our schedules around them. That we occasionally violated the routine I blamed, always apologetically, on Jan.

"It's almost noon," she said, without looking up at me.

"He probably hasn't noticed," I said. "My mom was the one who kept him on the straight and narrow."

She smiled at me.

"What?"

"He's wants me to smile more. So, I'm smiling."

"He wants everyone to smile more. It's a power-of-positive-thinking thing. He thinks smiling should be the baseline human expression. He probably thinks it's an evolutionary mistake that we didn't turn out that way."

"Just women," Jan said. "He doesn't smile."

"He sort of smiles."

"It's a grimace."

"Well, my mom did just die."

Jan put down the butter knife. She sighed. "I know. Honey, I'm sorry."

"It's okay. We'll work it out."

"I know. I love you."

"It's temporary. I'm going to start looking for a place. We'll work it out."

She was staring at the half-made sandwiches, with that smile—a doubtful one, I was sure—pasted to her face. Neither of us noticed my father until he said, "Something smells good."

He had brought his glass with him, and he put it down on the counter.

"I just want to reiterate," he said, clearing his throat, "that it is not my intention in any way, shape, or form to make either of you uncomfortable, or to ask you to alter your lives in any way to accommodate my presence."

Jan dug one nail under the other, alternately plucking and chewing. She only looked at her hands. My mother had been the one to notice the cues my father missed, to find something for him to do when Jan and I needed privacy, or to get work done, always with some apologetic line about needing my father for something, to which he would give a mock shrug. In a word, she had balanced him. And I was angry with Jan, for having so little faith that I would be able to do the same.

"It's all right, Dad. You're not putting us out. Really. Mom was right. The important thing is that we're all together." I was looking at Jan, she at her nails.

"I wish Welt was here," he said, his gaze lost somewhere beyond the kitchen. "She always knew what to do."

The next morning when I came downstairs my father was already awake. He was half-naked on the porch doing some kind of calisthenics, hands on his hips, bending at the waist and grunting. Then he started touching each knee with the opposite hand. The temperature had just crested fifty. I called good morning to him and asked if he wanted a cup of coffee. No answer. I knew he was supposed to limit himself to half a cup in the mornings, on his cardiologist's recommendation, and that had become my mother's policy. It would have to be my policy now. She had piloted his life firmly but tenderly into ripe old age. It was my responsibility now to maintain the course, even if it meant (I thought, somewhat overdramatically) that I had to lash myself to the helm.

I noticed something else lying on the wire table beside the binoculars, but it didn't really register until I had come back with our coffees and the pill organizer. I had prepared the pills in the kitchen late the night before, listening to him toss and turn on the futon in the meditation room, wondering how long it had been since he'd slept alone. My mother used to lay out his pajamas on his pillow.

And now here was my father, dressed knee to neck in a wetsuit. It was a sleek blue and black, highlighting the pallor of his shins and face, and the wispy gray hair on his head. There was something unsettlingly insectoid about his appearance, as though the suit were an exoskeleton, and he a white-headed, bipedal fly. Maybe I was just surprised he hadn't needed any help getting it on, and that he had effected this transformation in the time it had taken me to make coffee.

"Help me with these flippers," he said.

It took me a moment to piece it all together.

"Dad, please tell me you're not going into the pond."

"I'm going into the pond."

"Don't you want to wait to put these on until you're down there?"

"Not on your life."

"Dad, I would strongly counsel you against this."

But as I said all this I was already on one knee before him, like a suitor or a shoe salesman, our four hands working the flipper over his dry, chafed heel. The rubber squelched against his skin. It occurred to me that I had never touched his feet before.

This was how the story came out, over all the grunting and pulling around the flippers, of how he had bought the wetsuit for the pool, because the athletic club to which he and Welt had belonged failed to keep the water between eighty-three and eighty-six degrees, but when Welt had reported this to the cardiologist, he had been strictly forbidden from ever using the wetsuit again. So it had hung unused in the closet for the last five years.

"To hell with the cardiologist," my father said now. "He doesn't know his ass from a hole in the ground."

"Dad, the pond's a lot colder than the pool. We're not talking eighty-three to eighty-six degrees. It didn't even thaw until mid-March."

"That's what the wetsuit's for, Son."

I had watched him make his way around the house the day before, inspecting books and tchotchkes and pretty much anything that wasn't nailed down. His step was bowlegged and marionettish, and it quickly became apparent that anything left on the floor was a hazard. It seemed he could not judge distance, at least in relation to where to put his feet. I would think an object was well out of his way; but he would pause, raise one knee, and somehow step toward it, as though he really intended to destroy it, or be toppled himself in trying. Seeing him standing there in his wetsuit and flippers, I had a vision of our house in flaming ruins.

My father backed out the screen door and off the porch, feet shuffling in his flippers. He made a slow, backwards turn around the corner, and then started backwards down the slope toward the pond. I went out after him, shadowing him, though I resisted the impulse to take his hands. I kept expecting to have to—to see his eyes pop wide and his arms begin to cartwheel. We walked down the hill this way, like we were balancing something invisible between us; and perhaps because he could only take baby steps backwards, he negotiated the slope perfectly well, his gaze aimed at the patch of grass between us, or at my own slippered feet. He only spoke once, to ask if he was still going in the right direction.

Our pond was a little shorter than an Olympic swimming pool and maybe half as wide, with a crooked dock jutting out into the water partway down the near side. Weeds grew through the surface in bunches, a sign that I had to begin to attend to them, and in a couple of places leaves had rotted to form small floating islands of bright green scum. Otherwise, the water was dark and clear.

A small plastic boat leaned up against the old apple tree on the edge of the lawn, half-buried in last year's leaves. Its hull was gray from disuse; a jagged crack ran along one of the gunwales; the previous summer, hornets had nested in it. But I did not consider any of these things when my father instructed me to help him take it down. Together we eased it over, and then each of us took a mooring rope and began dragging it across the grass. We pushed the boat into the water, where it bobbed a few times and then rested. I leapt up onto the dock, feeling it bob once under me, and tied up the boat. My father sat down on the boards, swung his legs around so that his flippers dangled over the boat, and then eased himself down into it, just as he had done on the stairs, though here the drop was greater. While he settled in, I retrieved the oars for him, one of which was missing half a blade. Then I unwound the ropes from the bow and stern and dropped them in the boat, and gave a gentle sideways push. My father began to row.

I remembered quiet lunches and dinners on the porch with my parents, watching the pond. They had always admired the play of light on the water, the way it changed colors in the evenings, mirroring the colors of the nearest trees: willow, white birch, a single red maple. My mother would mention them, and my father would boom his assent. In the afternoons, Jan liked to float on the pond in an inflatable cushion, drinking cocktails and listening to NPR on a small radio set at the end of the dock. My mother had always mentioned how happy she looked, and my father would boom his assent. And then they would both urge me to get in the water, too. I had imagined a summer of the same, with just my father and Jan.

Once the boat was pointed in the right direction, it only took a few good tugs for him to reach the middle. He put the oars down and coasted. It was a beautiful morning. The birds were singing, the sun had crested the trees, steam was rising from the grass and from the roof of the garden well. When I turned back to the porch, I saw Jan.

"There's coffee," I said, when I had reached the screen.

"What on earth is he doing?"

"Rowing," I said. I heard a splash behind me. "Swimming," I said

"You're sure he can swim?"

"Oh, sure."

She rolled her eyes at me. "What if he's killing himself?"

I stared at her.

"Welt?" she said. "Remember? Your mom?"

My mouth was still hanging open when I turned back to the water. Together we waited for him to surface. The seconds were long. And then he appeared, a black-clad figure kicking slowly toward the southern irises, his face in the water.

He would be in the water before either of us was up. Some mornings I'd wake to the sound of him climbing into the boat: the hollow thunk of the oars, the plash of the paddles. Other days I slept right up until the moment he rolled into the pond. I never slept past that, and soon the passage of his body from the air to the water became the knife-edge between my sleeping and waking, as though I had really dreamt him. He slipped out of the dry world, out of my grasp, the moment I awoke.

I would bring him his coffee—a full cup now—and his pills, leave them at the end of the dock. When I came back an hour or two later, the coffee would be drunk and the pills untouched. I would chuck the pills in the water and bring the empty mug back to the house. The next day would be the same. I tried arguing, but he swore it had been a lot of worry about nothing; he had just never been able to tell Welt that, he had to let her have her way. I didn't say anything to Jan, until one day she spotted me throwing the pills in the pond. I tried to explain, but she just shook her head, frowning, and walked away.

At noon I'd call him in to lunch. We'd watch him come slowly up the hill, backwards, dripping, covered with weeds. He would squelch onto the porch, strip the wetsuit to his waist, and eat a cucumber sandwich, tearing at the bread with his gray teeth and gasping between bites like a man starving. His whole upper body was bright pink, as though he had been dipped head-first in dye, and the flesh of his hands was pruned. He never removed the flippers. In time, I would forget what his feet looked like without them.

My father had never really spoken about his time in the military as a young man; all I knew, or could remember, was that he had been stationed somewhere in Europe. But something about that time must have lain dormant in him, like a frozen beast waiting to thaw. Now, he could describe a sunset over Gibraltar with a level of detail that made me believe he was re-experiencing it as he spoke. The preternatural blueness of the Mediterranean around Cyprus; the rush of the water as he jumped with other men from his company into the warm, roiling waters of the Adriatic; the smell of some port slum in Italy . . . When I ventured to say what I was thinking—that he had never talked about his military experiences before, at least with the sense that they had been so formative—they had not been part of my childhood—he just waved his hand like I didn't know what I was talking about, or had never paid attention.

I did question the veracity of these memories, even as I feigned annoyance at his keeping them from me. Something in me wanted to corner him, to catch him in a lie, to run that booming voice aground—to force him to admit that the roiling Adriatic was really the pond on a windy day, Gibraltar was our angular gray house, the smell of the port slum was the muck on his body. Two things stopped me. First, I noticed that when he got caught up in these memories, or whatever they were, he was much less likely to say anything that rankled Jan. I had often found myself taking my father's side when they argued, and then feeling guilty about it later. Once the stories started, it was easier for Jan to slip away unnoticed, and she did so with a quiet authority, like a shoplifter.

The second thing was that I realized, no matter how baroque the event or winding the tale, eventually my mother would appear in it. They were just elaborate digressions to get to her, the center of the maze. And even if the story per se did not end there, there was always an addendum that included her. She, too, had seen the sunset over Gibraltar, if many years later. She, too, had swooned over the water around Cyprus, the color of a desert twilight. One day, when I finally decided to challenge him, my father looked at me and said, "Where do you think I met your mother?" I couldn't have been more surprised if he'd told me it had been in a Portuguese brothel. But there she was: no matter where in the world of his memory or imagination my father traveled, Welt had been fantastically, impossibly there.

And then abruptly he would say he had kept us long enough—he always used the plural, even though Jan had long since abandoned us. We had work to do, he boomed, even though he knew classes did not start again until after Labor Day. He would pull his wetsuit back up over his shoulders and squelch out. Reaching the pond, he would back straight off the bank into the water—it was only mornings that he bothered with the boat—do a barrelroll, and start kicking.

Jan and I did argue about it, at least early in the summer. It was too bizarre, it was too dangerous. The neighbors would talk. I had to call his doctor, a psychiatrist, one of his friends. But my father had no friends but Welt. Our neighbors, such as they were, hardly knew each other. His cardiologist was six hundred miles away, and besides, my father had already fired him, along with the rest of the medical profession. I told Jan he was happy. Hadn't she noticed the way he beamed at lunch, how animated he was? But she said there was something creepy, something unsettling, about his expression, which, she claimed, was fixed on the figure of my mother. "And have you looked at him?" she said. "Really, look at him." I said she was being unfair. I said it was temporary. "It's temporary," she said, "because one day soon you're going to find him floating belly-up."

I made a few half-hearted attempts to locate an affordable rest home, scrolled through the list of cardiologists at our medical group. They all looked the same. It was easier just to let things go on as they were. They were, in their own odd way, ideal. An opportunity for me to spend time with my father during his twilight years, the sort of thing my friends and colleagues, who were not fully apprised of the situation, told me I was blessed to have. An opportunity to do some long-overdue yard projects, too, half in an effort to mollify Jan, half to keep an eye on my father, or at least pretend to. Building stairs down to the creek. Laying gravel on the path through the woods. Weeding the pond. I used a metal rake with a rope tied to the handle. I would cast it out like a harpoon, let it sink for a few seconds, and then haul it back in, the rope cold and slimy in my grip, hoping to draw up a green pom-pom of weeds. Sometimes there would be a wriggling fish caught inside. Ferny, semi-translucent, garland-like, the weeds seemed to have arrived from another world; I understood that their beauty on land was only a fraction of their true beauty, which could only be appreciated underwater. The following day, when the water had drained from the stacks I had made along the bank, they would be gray and brittle, and light as paper as I picked them up with a pitchfork. They left marks like scorches on the grass.

It was tedious work, and I weeded that summer like I was doing penance, watching over my father as if he were a child at the beach. Eventually he did come to seem to me like the dream of the child Jan and I had never had, the child whose absence my parents had said would force us apart, in just the way my presence had welded them together. But though I spent all day with him, I still sometimes felt like I was neglecting him, even abusing him. I had an irrational fear of braining him with the rake. I imagined him as a leviathan I was trying to catch, if I could just bring myself to aim true. He nibbled at the rind of my conscience, and each time I looked to him, I was afraid to find him belly-up, as per Jan's omen. And yet, I refused to do anything about it; and my disinclination to intervene, to truly change things rather than simply manage them as they were, caused everything to fall under enchantment. We inhabited a static, idyllic world. Nothing could happen to him, so long as it lasted.

In the evenings, when he came up to the house, I would be alone on the porch, the leftovers of whatever Jan had cooked for dinner spread upon the wire table. She would be in bed; she went to bed earlier and earlier as the summer wore on, and came outside less and less. Once, when she came across my father resting in the irises, she shrieked as if she had seen a snake. There was something uncanny about him. Watching him approach back-first, for example: his face transformed into a featureless gray mottle, his joints all bent the wrong way, and his feet black knobs with crests grown from the heels. But he hardly seemed worth shrieking over, sitting there in his faded wetsuit, in the evening glow, a faraway expression on his face, speaking in a voice that boomed gently, like thunder heard from another valley, about Gibraltar, or the roiling Adriatic, or the miraculously-colored fish that swam in and out of the hulls of sunken ironsides, while I picked the yellow tendrils of weeds that hung ceremoniously from his shoulders, like epaulettes.

And then one noon, when I went to bring him his sandwich, I found him sitting on the bank by the dock, panting. As I came up beside him, he raised one hand, an imperious hand that trembled ever so slightly.

"Important announcement," he said.

I waited for him to catch his breath.

"I've found Welt," he said.

I put the sandwich on the grass. I think I said, "Oh?"

"It took a while." Pant. "Longer than I expected. Tough out there."

"Well," I said, "mission accomplished, I guess. Congratulations, Dad. Does that mean you're coming inside now?"

That look on his face again.

"Accomplished?" he barked. "That was phase one."

"I see," I said. "Phase one. What's phase two?"

He took a bite of the sandwich, took his time chewing. He never talked with his mouth full.

"Please inform Jan," he said. "And please apologize for my ignoring her. I realize I'm not being a very good guest. I hope she understands."

With that he scooted around and crabwalked backwards into the water again, leaving the rest of his sandwich uneaten on the bank.

"In the pond?" Jan said.

"I guess so. Where else?"

"How does she look? Old, young?"

"He didn't say."

"Have you called somebody?"

"Who do you want me to call?"

"Honey, your dad thinks your dead mother is in our pond. Do you think just maybe he's planning to join her?"

"Why do you always have to be so negative?"

"I'm not being negative, I'm being realistic. How much longer do you think he can make it out there? It's almost August."

"Problem solved, then. He'll have to come inside."

I could feel her stare, the slight shift in the bedclothes. I sighed.

"All right. What do you want me to do?"

"What do I want you to do? Have you done anything? Have you lifted a finger or taken any responsibility at all? God, you're worse than him. You're absolutely helpless. Where's Welt when you need her?"

"In the pond, apparently. Jan, I think he's happy . . . "

"And what about me? Am I happy? She-who-doesn't-smile often enough, broadly enough?"

"At least he doesn't follow you around the kitchen reading labels aloud anymore. He doesn't even stretch out on the bank. Remember? 'Oh, honey, old people aren't supposed to be able to bend their bodies that way. He's too *limber*.'"

"You're missing the point."

"When was the last time you even saw him in the meditation room during the day? Wasn't that our number-one concern? Now you can read in there all day if you want, and nobody's going to bother you."

"Are you listening to yourself?"

I was. My voice had taken on a hysterical edge, at once defensive and self-righteous, the voice of someone brandishing a wound in front of a judge

"He barely comes inside," I went on, more quietly. "He has effectively vacated the premises."

"I preferred it when he was reading labels. This freaks me out."

"Clearly. It's why you barricade yourself inside all day. Since when do you lock the front door when we're home?"

"Since your dad decided to play Creature from the Black Lagoon, maybe?"

"Please."

"It's not just me. All nature is terrified of him. Mrs. Jowry's cats puff up and hiss every time they see him coming. Have you seen a single animal on the property since this all started? Rabbits, birds? The heron? Has the heron come by once this summer?"

"Jan."

"The garden's going all to seed. And I used to float. Remember? You'd bring me a cocktail, sit on the end of the dock with your feet in the water? We'd talk? Remember? Remember the mojitos last summer?"

"We can do that again."

"With the Swamp Thing out there?"

"Fine, I'll tell him he can only swim until noon. I'll tell him has to come up to the porch for lunch. I'll call someone to take him off to the funny farm," I said, warming to my own resolve, "so he can get some real drugs and be with Welt all the time."

"No, you won't. You're going to let things go on just like they have. He'll spawn with Welt, or God knows what, and you're going to stand there, watching."

I wanted to tell her about how, when he came inside in the evenings, squelching around the first floor, I was the one shuffling behind him with towels on my feet. I was the one who had stored the rugs, perennially damp, and a hazard every time he bunched one trying to traverse it. I was the one leaving lunch at the end of the dock every day, and bringing him coffee in the mornings. That he hardly ate or drank anything anymore didn't seem worth mentioning. What mattered was that I had adapted, I was trying to make things work for us, while she had withdrawn, the gesture of picking at her nails writ large.

Jan entwined herself around me, vine on stump. "I'm trying," I said, weakly. "I really am . . . "

It was all I could say. She said she knew, that she was sorry. That she loved me. She kissed my eyelids.

"This isn't about me," she murmured. "I shouldn't have brought that stuff up. It's not even about him, not anymore. It's about you. I'm worried about you."

I felt her heart beating against mine. "Okay," I whispered.

Then she whispered, "Remember *The Blob*?"

" . . . The movie?"

"Yeah. The movie. Remember how they got rid of it?"

" . . . Remind me."

"They froze it and carried it to the Arctic," she whispered.

"My father is not *The Blob*," I whispered.

She sighed in my ear. "It's a metaphor. Jesus, you're such a child sometimes."

"My father," I said, with rising indignation, "is fauna."

Jan held onto me tightly, her breath hot on the lobe of my ear.

"Why do you think people move to Florida when they retire? Have you never thought about it? Cold is a weapon."

That night I dreamed not of my father, but my mother. I hadn't dreamed of her since the funeral. I was weeding the pond, and my father was floating. I snagged what I thought was a bunch of weeds and started to haul them in. But when I hefted them onto the bank, they were heavy with something else. I pulled weeds aside, like they were vines grown over a headstone, until I found my mother. Only it wasn't her, it was an amazing effigy of her, with twigs for bones and weeds for capillaries, hair made of rotted leaves, and walnuts for eyes. It was like one of those model toys of the human body, with transparent skin and removable plastic organs. I stared at it until I expected it to come to life—and so it did, smiled and embraced me, a cold, weak embrace I could not return. And yet it clung, or caught to me, like a creeper with spines. My struggle to free myself became a struggle to wake, and came at the price of the Welt-effigy, which collapsed into a pile of sticks and leaves and mud. Jan was asleep beside me. My father was in the pond.

August. I did no work; I grew contemplative, staring down into the water, at the patient fish with their tails swaying like my father's feet, quiet as the heron. The water was limpidly clear from all my weeding, and I felt that I had done no small part for my father's mission, whatever it was now. He had never spoken of it again. In fact, he barely spoke at all. How could he, when he barely left the water? He no longer came up to the porch for dinner. He spent the whole day floating in the same spot, as much a fixture of the yard as the red maple. The only way I could determine he was still alive was by seeing a fin move, or bubbles appear around his head. If he was motionless for too long, I threw pebbles at him, and then slightly larger stones if I failed to get a reaction. When a stone connected, his leg would kick as if he had received a jolt from a galvanic battery. I would have used a bamboo pole instead, except that he no longer floated within reach of the dock.

The days were growing noticeably shorter, the nights colder. Coming up to the house at dusk, I would find the screen door latched. Jan would come downstairs with a flashlight to let me in. The dinner leftovers were covered in foil on the kitchen table. She would sit silently across from me, my father fallen between us like a curtain. I could no longer look at her, pitying me, or blaming me. I ate silently, and ate everything, making sure to leave nothing for him. No more coffee in the morning or sandwiches at noon. I have no idea what he ate, if he ate. But later at night, lying in bed, we would hear the porch door slam, and then the inside door squeak open; we would listen to him squelching around the first floor. It seemed an inordinate amount of time, an inordinate number of steps, before he reached the meditation room. Some nights he was more restless than others, and it might be a full half-hour before he settled down. We would listen, holding our breaths, as though we expected at any moment to hear his stertorous breath as he crabwalked up the stairs, to see his backside appear in the bedroom doorway.

I could no longer deny that he was changing. The remains of his wetsuit hung off him like a skin he had begun to shed. At once pruned and bloated, he had taken on a pale green hue, my father had, though in a few places the weeds had stained him an orange-yellow, almost a dull gold. Moss had grown in the depressions of his ribcage, as on the shell of a turtle. His eyes shone dully, like old coins; I was not convinced he could still see through them, at least outside of the water. And just as I knew the weeds looked different, looked beautiful, inside the water, so I knew that, while on land my father might have looked odd, even troubling, it was only in the pond that the changes made sense. It was not age; these were not the so-called ravages of time. Rather, he was changing laterally, in time's interstices—the cracks and fissures between sedimentary layers, where all our fabled common ancestors lived.

By early September the temperature had begun dipping into the forties at night, though it would be at least another month before the first frost. Was my father growing a thicker skin to survive the winter? Perhaps he had a burrow under the bank, like a muskrat, and was preparing to hibernate. Perhaps his metamorphosis was into something closer to flora: he would return in the spring, permanent in his own way, but so different that he would no longer be able to see or sense me. It would be up to me to recognize him. Or perhaps he had shriveled like a leaf—it was the reason he floated so effortlessly—and I could have easily lifted him out with the skimmer, if only I could have reached him. Even when he rested in the irises, we spoke so little that I began to wonder if he was losing the power of speech. He seemed to need nothing now, least of all me. But I needed him—we both did, Jan and I, though I could not define precisely how.

And then one evening we didn't hear him come inside. The bed in the meditation room was damp, empty but for weeds. The pond was empty, its black surface undisturbed. I ran down the hill in my pajamas, calling his name. Jan called mine from the window. A few moments later, tramping about in the irises, I almost stumbled over his recumbent form. I should have known he would be here, in his favorite resting spot, the place where the weak currents carried him over the course of the day, where he bedded down every evening in a nest of mashed petals and leaves. Stepping back, I was just able to make out his form against the fanning leaves, themselves dark spines against an infinitesimally lighter sky.

"Dad? Don't you want to come inside?"

Now that my heart had settled, I could hear him breathing, a gentle wheeze under the chirping late-summer frogs.

He said, "I'm fine here." Quietly, but in a voice still very much his own. "It's supposed to rain tonight," I said.

I hadn't looked at the weather. The sky was clear, and the moon was just a sliver, barely brighter than the stars.

"It's okay," he said, "I'm comfortable."

I listened to him wheeze, and to the frogs surrounding me, singing the end of summer.

Then he said, "Don't worry about me. I'm fine here. You go on."

I slept on the dock that night, and every night thereafter. The frogs fell silent, and the house seemed as far away as the moon, and then farther; because though the moon grew slowly night by night, the house never changed, and so it seemed to recede as the moon drew nearer.

Standing in the window like a sailor's widow, Jan was as small as a candle. She called to me, but I did not come, and in time I stopped hearing her, and then seeing her, except in the evenings, when she came out to leave a bowl of soup or hot rice at the other end of the dock. Only once that I can remember did she walk out to me, and caress my cheek, and kiss my forehead, as though I were suffering a fever, fighting an illness for which she could offer no more than consolation.

My father seemed to grow more distant, too. Perhaps it was the light, at least during the day, the angle of the sun dazzling the water. At night he seemed to float in space, a tetherless astronaut adrift in the currents of the void. Then he began to flash, like a beacon from a lighthouse, there, not there, and then there again. At first I thought my attention must have drifted long enough for him to have had time to kick quietly to the southern irises. But something told me to count. I decided that if he did not reappear by fifteen, I would be forced to do something, I didn't know what. Stab the water with a bamboo pole in the place where I had last seen him? Cast the weeding rake into the water? Imagining what I might do made me count past fifteen. I thought I must have counted too quickly, so I started again, making sure to mutter "one thousand" before each number.

On ten he resurfaced, almost silently. He was still except for his head, which he raised every few seconds to breathe. Then I saw it happen: his back hunched, he doubled over in the water, and he kicked his scrawny legs up in the air, flippers noiselessly suspended for a few moments, before going down in a cloud of bubbles.

This went on all through September. I used up my sick days, while Jan took advantage to leave work early when she could, or sometimes just call out, pushing off part of her load onto one of the more accommodating and impressionable younger sisters. Arriving at home, she would find me, as ever, at the end of the dock, watching my father's shadow descend, flipper-feet disappearing last. Even on the brightest days, where I could see through to the tops of the weeds, he went deep enough that he vanished entirely. I had begun to imagine all the awful things that might happen to him while he was down there, from getting snagged in the weeds, to having a dizzy spell and not being able to tell the direction of the surface, to simply miscalculating and running out of air. But the longer this went on, the longer he was able to go without surfacing. Instead, I imagined him learning through patient trial and error to breathe underwater. I thought again of hibernation, of his blood growing viscous and freezing with the earth. Each time he returned to the surface, there would be just a little less of him.

Leaves dotted the water. Some of them landed on him. I heard Jan's voice calling me from the window, from the porch, from the top of the lawn, from the other end of the dock. How could I leave now, with him on the point of leaving me? And yet, how would I know when he had left? At what number, at what point in our short little lives, are we supposed to stop thinking *longer*, and start thinking *eternity*?

But one cold afternoon I did know, just like I knew the canoes the leaves made, the mottled red of the maple across the pond, the elephantine skin of my own drawn-up knees. I called for Jan, until she appeared in the window, on the porch, at the top of the lawn. I watched her make the half-circle around the pond to the garden gate, where she untied the rope from the weeding rake and brought it to me, helped me to tie it around my waist. She stepped on the other end. If anything happened, I was supposed to tug.

One kiss, and then a hard push.

The water wasn't as cold as I thought it would be. Something about the depth of the pond—twelve feet, supposedly, at its deepest point—must have helped to stabilize the temperature. It was the same depth as the diving tank of the pool in the town where I had grown up. Yet, the pond seemed deeper, much deeper, the pressure on my ears that much greater. Maybe it was just the murkiness of the water. Looking up, I could just make out Jan's dim outline wavering on the surface.

The real problem, though, was that I couldn't tell if I had reached the bottom. There seemed to be no bottom. The silt went on and on, so fine that, for an unreasonable distance, it was neither water nor earth, but something between the two. I found myself half-walking, half-swimming in a pitch-black gelatin. Legs buried in the watery silt, arms and face swathed in weeds I could feel but not see, I understood how justified had been my fear that my father could become lost or trapped down here.

I kicked free, came up for air.

"Anything?" Jan called.

I shook my head, gasping. The rope, I noticed, was tied around her waist. She gave it a few short, sharp tugs, as for practice.

The second time I thought the pond would seem less deep, but the reverse was true. Because I didn't have the impetus of the jump, I thought, or because I had found some unmapped trench in the blind geography of that bottomless bottom—whatever the case, down and down I went. I was buffeted by fish, corkscrewed by powerful currents; weeds caught at my arms and legs, as though to avenge themselves.

And then I found him, knocked into his bones and flesh, or he into mine. He threw his arms around me, and I around him, and we danced this way, like astronauts. Except it wasn't just him; my mother was here, too, just as he had said she was. We were all here, the three of us, dancing this slow dance together. I saw her face as it had appeared in the coffin, and I knew now what his flesh felt like: like the flesh of my dead mother's face. I saw the pictures, the two of them, always together—except I was in those pictures now, between them. I had cut myself out in my memory, but I was still there, in the contours of my absence. Now it was my father who filled that space, a tenuous last link between us. His had been a slow turning, like a shadow on a sundial, toward this other world. He had spent the summer excavating his own grave, without tools, without aid. But with an audience: Jan, watching from afar; and I, floating on the margins, so eager to fit myself back into that space between them, beside her, pressed up against her.

I was almost out of air when I reached behind me to tug on the rope. Then, my arms still wrapped around their narrow trunks, fingers tightly laced, I started to kick.

I didn't panic, at least not at first. Jan did tug back, but weakly. There was no bottom to push off of. And there was a certain amount of inertia to overcome. Still, we went nowhere—or, rather, we went down. I was sure that we were all sinking together into ever-siltier depths, like a family trapped in the cabin of a torpedoed ship, huddled together in prayer. I began to swallow convulsively, as though I could make air this way, kicking and squirming, my whole body a tail. Still I was sure we went on sinking.

When at last I understood that I could not bring them up, I drew my knees to my chest and planted my feet on theirs, the only other solid thing down here; and I pushed, until I felt their grip break. My legs followed through; they sank; I rose, clawing my way toward the surface and Jan.

That first breath. It was the sort you take when you've exhausted yourself from crying, sucking down all that cold air just so you can start over again.

I'm out gathering kindling, splitting wood and stacking it behind the garage. Jan is raking by the pond. The other day, the red maple dumped all its leaves, as though something had terrified it. The ground is white with frost; the pond has a thin skein of ice over it; one of Jan's floats is frozen there. It's been a cold November, everything bright and still, and silent when we pause, an ideal paralysis that's the closest the earth comes to heaven.

I hear the geese almost a minute before the first ones appear over the northernmost trees. A distant rumor, a few lonely honks. I put down the halves of a log I've just split, gently, as though, were I to drop them, I risked frightening the geese away. I've been waiting for their visit, though I didn't know it. They unfurl over the horizon, more and more, until they own the sky above me—fifty, maybe more, in a few broken Vs, a pattern like the notches in a piano roll, cranked over us in some Ptolemaic mock-up of earth and sky. The honking rises to a din, and each goose is an instrument, and each goose is a will. I look briefly at Jan, who is watching, rake poised in both hands. It lasts just long enough, just as long as it needs to—just as long as I need it to—and then they're leaving, diminishing. I listen for a long time after the hindmost disappear over the southern trees, savoring their calls like the last trace of a flavor dissolving on the tongue.

THE TECHNOLOGIES
OF PUCKS

MORNINGS AND EVENINGS, ON THEIR WAY TO AND FROM THE POND, the boys would hear the old Tilson woman calling to her cat. She would stand on the front step of her little red house, the flower-print dress she wore no matter the weather hanging from her shoulders like a sack, her legs swollen and gnarled, and, holding the bowl out toward the white propane tank like it was an offering, ululate loudly, rest, repeat. Then she would put the bowl down and go inside. It was the only time anyone ever saw her, except perhaps when she peered around a half-drawn curtain at some passerby, like an animal from its burrow. No one knew exactly how old she was; the most reliable estimates put her a few years shy of a hundred. Her son, who came by to check on her every few days, was guarded about his mother's age.

As for the cat, white with a black mark under its chin, no one could remember the last time they'd seen it, and it was widely believed to be dead. There were in fact a number of people who claimed to have run it over—put the thing out of its misery, they snickered, through the nicotine haze at the diner; for what creature would want to go through life at the eerie beck and call of that old wretch?

Her call would break suddenly upon the ch, ch, ch of their boots as they followed the grey scramble of their own tracks through the snow. They were ruddy with cold, lips and fledgling beards frozen stiff with snot, bright in their jerseys as winter birds. Sticks over their shoulders, skates tied to the ends, they looked more like hobos or drifters than the natural-born sons of this valley. The old men who hung around the VFW had said it was going to be this kind of a winter: the kind the valley hadn't seen in twenty years, the kind it had forgotten existed; the kind that had been typical when *they* were boys. They had predicted it from the caterpillars—not by how hairy they were, but by their coloring: the ratio of yellow or white to black, the width and spacing of their stripes. Word had trickled down to the boys, three generations their junior, who didn't know whether to believe them. Barnabases, their generic name for any old man, after one of the valley's first settlers, were prone to tell tales. Their fathers all said so. But then to their fathers, a hard winter meant little more than extra money from plowing and towing, and a few extra cords of wood sold. To the boys, the caterpillars looked just the same, match-box Chinese dragons, the sort they paraded through the streets with firecrackers, at least on TV.

When the first snow failed to come early, or even on time, and the first few powdery inches melted away in a mild early December, the caterpillar story became the butt of their jokes. It was a different world, after all. Some of those men were old enough to remember the highway going in; some of them had even worked on it during the administration of Dwight D. Eisenhower. The power lines had come later, a swathe almost as wide as the highway cut right through their land; they would reminisce about the fight against it with Korea-like nostalgia. They knew the valley as it had been before their sons and grandsons, the boys' fathers and grandfathers, had started to drift away to the gas wells up north, or to the business route that jughandled from the highway south. Those of them who could get work, anyway; those who couldn't went further, and usually didn't come back. They talked about the valley when the land had been worth something for itself, instead of for what was hidden underneath it, before all the leasing and parceling and selling off had pitted neighbors against each other as fiercely as the struggle against the power lines had once united them. All that land lay fallow now, and still undeveloped, its owners waiting. Yes, it was a different world. Nobody read caterpillars anymore. But it beat the hell out of reading books. And then maybe it wasn't the Barnabases at all. Because the caterpillars were even older than the Barnabases, and if the Barnabases couldn't keep up how was a caterpillar supposed to?

They remembered the caterpillars—and maybe their fathers did, too—when the first big snow came in mid-December, knocking out the power, the valley ahum with generators, and then the cold snap that drove the temperature down into the single digits for a solid week. It was then they started going to the Tilson pond every day to observe the changes. They called it the Tilson pond, although they were honestly unsure who the land past the power lines belonged to. It was a safe bet. Once upon a time, one Tilson or another had owned a quarter of the valley; the name, Tilson, was well represented by a clutch of stones in the old graveyard behind the defunct Methodist church. Barnabas had been a Tilson, probably still was. The stones were set off by chains, some decorated with artificial flowers and flags, and the lawn around them was always mowed, although many of the inscriptions were too worn to read. The stones were better for sitting on, anyway, or for smoking on, or for trying sex behind, while someone else looked out from the bed of the pickup that sat in the church driveway on eternally flat tires. They had all looked through the one unshuttered window of the church at one time or another, too, and but for the one who would never say what he had seen, they had all seen the same thing: retired farm machinery, rusted tools; the kinds of things people pulled in off the highway to buy for antiques.

It was their pond, anyway. They never asked anyone's permission to fish in the summer and skate in the winter, and even on days when the son's truck was parked piled high with firewood in the old lady's driveway no one ever chased them off, and nobody but them ever came out as far as the pond. As for the no-trespassing and private-property signs—the unsigned ones, presumed to belong to the Tilsons; the ones posted by the local gun club; the ones for the downstate utility and three different gas companies, none of them local—and the for-sale signs decorated with bright realtors' logos, and the one sign alerting them that they were on state parkland, so old and riddled with bullet holes as to be almost illegible—they all meant as much or as little, which is to say, nothing. They were like arcane messages from another world, a world the boys firmly believed they were not part of, that they moved around, skirting its edges, although sometimes they believed they could hear it scraping against their own. Did the ghosts of the Barnabases trespass when they rose up at night to possess the deer that traipsed through the graveyard, and that the boys sometimes spooked as they passed, ghostly white tails flashing in the moonlight? Did the turkeys, the raccoons, the rabbits trespass in their daily perambulations? Then how could they? They meant as much as the deer did, and read as little. And then it might occur to them that their fathers hunted those deer, and they sometimes went along. Some days they brought twenty-twos along with them and shot at a stray rabbit or bird, mostly to listen to the report die away into silence. They tugged fish out of the Tilson pond in summers without thinking who but God they belonged to. They trekked underneath hunters' roosts, and one day they had stumbled upon a hide, gleaming orange and green like a medallion, one side shingled with leaves. They surrounded it like it was a fallen meteor. Walking again, they said things to each other like: You think a deer is really fooled by that? They're none too smart. They don't see too good either. Could've fooled me. Well, maybe you should watch out my old man doesn't shoot you. You're none too smart either. Oh, snap. Ch, ch, ch.

There were stone walls everywhere, low and half-toppled, half-buried in snow, vestigial boundary lines from some long-extinct apportioning. The boys clambered over them, crossing sometimes in file through the notches where the stones had all tumbled down, and sometimes abreast, like a platoon fording a river, sticks held over their heads in both hands like rifles. Following their own tracks, they crossed those of the deer, and turkeys, and rabbits, and Mr. Barrow's thirteen-year-old shepherd dog. They wound between the bare oak and poplar and elm, stepping over fallen trunks, some with the bark shorn away, or ducking under snow-slung branches. Sometimes as they walked they heard a branch crack and fall with a whump. Halfway up the mountain they intersected with a driveway, which they followed for a full turn, then cut through more woods to the clearing for the power lines. They walked along the utility road until they came upon a peculiar-looking boulder whose concave side was a sheet of ice. Here they left the road, clambered over ledge after upended ledge of jagged granite until they reached the ridge.

Standing atop a weathered American flag painted on the rock, they could see the low flat humps of the further Adirondacks like the backs of whales, and they could follow the rise and fall of the utility towers through the lighter green track across the hillsides into the distance. Though they could not see the highway, they could hear it better from here than anywhere else, especially when the tankers barrelled up and down it in convoys of six or seven. Occasionally they would hear the distant reports from the gas wells, the low rumble through the hills, like a war they were expected to attend when they were old enough to enlist, and for which they were even now in training. Everyone had someone working up there, just like everyone had someone in the service, or in one of the prisons an hour to the south. The wells had drawn the sons of the sons of the farmers north, had pumped them out of the soil as heedlessly and violently as they did the gas. Father and uncles, brothers old enough to have dropped out. They came home most weekends, sometimes for longer. A couple of the boys had ridden up there with them: land like the surface of the moon, explosions that made the earth seize up, jets of flame high up into the night sky like solar flares, the silhouettes of men huddled inside of them, hangars of trucks filled with water, water, water, amazing quantities of water, and a smell that stayed on their clothes long after they'd come back. In a couple of years they'd be old enough to follow. But in a couple of years, the wells would be here—and it was about time, or so most people said.

Beyond the ridge the trail dropped down into a high meadow, stakes poking up here and there through the snow. The woods on this side were mostly pine, at least until the boys got close enough to the stream to hear the water. They followed it, watching the current through the warped, semi-transparent pane of ice frozen over most of its surface, down into a small hollow: the pond, a rough ellipse fifty yards wide on its major axis. Each morning during the week of the cold snap its surface would be changed. A sheet of ice covering the eastern half, the water lapping it like a shore, then spreading to cover the whole pond, so thin they could send shock waves across it by tapping the edges with their boots, the water sloshing against the just-frozen edges. They threw pebbles, listened to them chirp and echo as they disappeared into the grey, broke the ice with sticks, or with their feet—a sudden asterisk—just for the eerie pleasure of feeling them go through, the other planted safely on the bank. Over the next days the sheet whitened from its middle out, growing more opaque as it thickened, like a cataract, took a firmer grasp of the banks, and crept entirely over the little pools by the inlet and outlet. They got fist-sized stones, and on the count of three, hurled them as high and far as they could—not to compete for distance, but to mark whether the stones would plunge through, or even crack the surface. On the morning the stones bounced a few times, barely chipping the ice, they went back home, to their toolsheds or mudrooms or garages, and pulled the handed-down skates off their pegs, the blades all freckled with rust, the boots filled with cobwebs. They met up again at the house of a Barnabas who had used to build sleighs, who watched them blindly while they took turns at the grinding wheel, blades whining like boards in a sawmill, hot when the boys ran their thumbs along the metal.

At the end of the snap the temperature shot up ten degrees, and it snowed lightly overnight, coating the pond with an inch of powder. Early the next morning they hung their skates over their shovels and push brooms and marched up the mountain again, saying hut, hut, hut. One carried a battery-powered drill, and spent the hike pointing the bit at the boy in front of him and pressing the trigger. Another brought an auger. They were always hesitant on the first day—that was normal—but this season it was magnified by the early freeze. They had sounded the Tilson pond two summers before, from a canoe they had humped out, and needed little to remind them that there was between twelve and twenty feet of cold water beneath the ice, where the sunnies and the bass still wounded by their hooks turned slow circles in the dark. The voices of their parents rang in their ears, too, as they stood along the south bank staring out at the veil of snow. Their fathers would have had them stay away entirely. But they were too preoccupied, or too tired, or too drunk, or too ornery about something unrelated to the boys. Their mothers loaded them down with injunctions: Bundle up. Look out for each other. Take the auger, the drill, the ice claws, the ladder. Get milk, sugar, bread, butter, spaghetti sauce. Dinner's at six, six-thirty, seven. Don't do anything silly, stupid, crazy, idiotic. Don't make dares. Don't take dares. Don't try to impress anybody. Are there going to be girls there? Use your head. Don't just walk out there like a dummy. That's how Anthony drowned. Remember Tony?

Of course they remembered Tony. He had fallen through the ice and drowned. At least, that was what they had determined after the fact; they hadn't found the body until spring, blue-grey in his sodden coat, skates still strapped to his feet. Turned out he hadn't lit out for the City after all, whatever all the other kids were doing. He wouldn't have lasted a minute before going under.

It had happened right around the time they were born. Tony had been quite a bit older than they were now when it had happened, but to their mothers it just made them that much more vulnerable. So they told their mothers what they wanted to hear: that Tony had been stupid, for going out alone, for getting drunk, or whatever he had done wrong. They promised not to be like Tony. But when they were out there on the ice, they thought they understood Tony in a way their mothers didn't, or didn't anymore. Or maybe they did, and that was what made them nervous. Why he had come out alone. Why he'd gone out too early, or stayed too late. Why he would have skated too near thin ice. It had to be his fault; the alternative was too frightening. They couldn't explain it, the bright, hypnotic beauty of the ice, the ricocheting sunlight. It called to you. Tony. He would have been in his thirties now, somebody's father, his son a friend at school, one of them. They skated with this ghostly boy, felt his presence on the ice, just as they felt Tony's under it.

Because the body had been poled out of the lake a dozen miles downstream it was easy to extrapolate from the story to make it a lesson about all ponds. The boys didn't believe it had happened at the Tilson pond—or, if it had, they didn't believe the Tilson pond would do such a thing to them. Still, that first step. The snow helped a little, because they were not entirely sure whether they stood on hard ground or over water. They waited until one got the nerve to take another few steps, the shoreline visible now as a slight hump behind him; and then a third, carrying the drill, a step beyond him, dragging his feet, leaving dark skids in the snow. Even though they knew the bottom dropped precipitously, they figured that nothing could happen to them just a few arm-lengths from the bank. The one with the drill dropped to his knees, brushed away the snow to reveal a dark oval. The bit whined as it cut, the rest watching, a few still from the bank. It was four inches from the tip of the bit to the housing. When the threading had entirely disappeared in the ice, the boy pulled it out and stared down into the cleanly-bored hole, shavings at the bottom, and announced his failure to break through. In the meantime, the boy with the auger had started turning the handle, and the rest began to fan out onto the ice. And then one who up until that moment had been standing on the bank walked out toward the humps of the buried stones. He walked like one anointed, or possessed, a few other boys following him in a broken V. Near the middle he paused; the boys faced each other across a wide expanse of snow-covered ice, like stones themselves, each half-expecting the other to fall through, as though each was only buoyed by the others' half-belief, or even more, by their presence, their role as witnesses. They might have been walking on water, though it looked more like cloud. Then the boy with the auger cried out he'd hit a gusher; the water came up and puddled on the ice, like he had made a hole in the bottom of a boat, and the entire sheet was in danger of sinking. Five inches, he barked. Minimum. The ones standing out on the middle of the ice broke into smiles, and then started jumping up and down. Even as they slipped and fell, they felt light as air.

They raced back to the bank for their skates, shovels, brooms. Suddenly the pond was a whir of noise and activity, shovels scraping across the ice, the blades of the skates carving. One started a track along the bank, shovel bumping over the leaves frozen into the surface. The rest plowed in rows straight across, holding their shovels at an angle like plow-blades, so that the leading edge left only a thin line of powder behind, and most of the snow sloughed off the dragging one. Another boy would swoop in behind to handle the sloughed-off snow, shovel angled the same way, and then another behind him. They worked this way in both directions, raising their blades to dump the accumulated snow when they were near enough to the banks, and forming little levees by the inlet and outlet, about ten feet from the edges of the small pools. Occasionally the stones they had hurled would rattle into their blades, or trip them up if they had stuck. These had to be chiseled out. When they got tired of the routine, they tried locking arms with a couple of partners and making a single long plow from the blades of a few shovels, or skating with two shovels, one in each hand, trying to keep the blades together and angled away from each other. The brooms came in after, first wooden side down to push off the excess snow, then the bristles, dabbing and pushing, dabbing and pushing, so that a pattern of squares emerged as they moved across the ice. It was a good warm-up and reminder for their muscles, skating with the shovels, dabbing with the brooms, stopping short at the banks to dump the snow, turning in tight circles to begin another row. Sometimes the blades of their shovels would clash, hook, send them spinning down onto the ice. The boys would spring up and fence clumsily, until one went back to plowing, leaving the other to listen to the skates and shovels, and the sound of his own breath, and maybe the wind in the pines, and the peep of a winter bird.

It took them half an hour to strip away the veil hiding the ice, and but for a bit of horseplay with the shovels they worked without pause or distraction. It was as though they were polishing a great mirror for some god to admire itself in. What with the ice revealed, and the morning quiet, and the new warmth as the sun crested the treetops and made the ice a sea of light, what choice did they really have about how to spend the rest of their morning? Most of the surface was a scuffed, opaque white, but there were patches of perfectly smooth blackness, all the more wondrous for their relative rarity. Each was like the window of a display cabinet in some pond museum. Looking through, they could see the weeds trailing up from the dark bottom, motionless as a diorama, which they kept expecting some drowsy, meandering fish to animate ... or perhaps Tony, blue-grey but young as them, floating by face-up just under the ice, mouth moving silently as a fish's. There were bubbles by the millions, clouds of them like galaxial dust, others large as fists, frozen into trails and tendrils, like the arms of squids. In one place the ice had frozen a bubble that looked just like a glass urchin. They skated slowly over these patches, elbows on their knees, blades wobbling ever so slightly. Passing silently, the surface below firm but invisible, they had the sensation of gliding through a void, glimpsing a hidden world below before the white opaqueness obscured it again, like a bank of cloud.

The silent wonder didn't last long. Soon they were racing in a clockwise oval, shouldering and elbowing each other, or skating full-speed at one another, locking arms at the last moment to spin a tight circle before breaking apart and plummeting to the ice, or making slapdash hurdles out of stacked shovels and brooms. They were clumsy compared to how they would be a month from now, but felt light as birds compared to their earthbound selves of an hour before. By the time they thought to leave, the sun had tracked halfway across the pond low over the trees. A miracle that they didn't stay until nightfall. But then they were hungry, and figured that if they hustled a little they might make it for lunch at the cafeteria, for what it was worth. School might have been an ordeal, except that there was something so satisfying about walking in with the day already half-over, about the loud clatter of the skates as they deposited them in their lockers, just to make sure the teachers and other students heard them, and then shambling off together toward the cafeteria to eat silently at the same table, aware of all the eyes upon them, smiling at each other, laughing giddily when one of them ululated like the old lady, and another meowed, before wandering off in two or three different directions to math or reading or social studies, to doze off to the hiss and ping of the radiators and the drone of the teachers' voices in the heavy, institutional warmth. By the end of the day they could hardly muster the energy to rise from their desks. They walked in a half-stoop on numb, ragged stumps for feet, the muscles in their legs barely able to push them forward. At home, their mothers teased them that they looked like old-timers. But even sore, or maybe because of it, they went to bed feeling weightless, and dreamt of a field of ice black as pitch on which they moved noiselessly and at such speed that the pondside trees became a blur and not even the scant few birds could keep up with them.

They limbered up quickly, grew fast and confident, forgot the hardness of the ice and the water beneath it. Their bodies remembered everything: how to go backwards as easily as forwards, make tight turns in either direction, or stop short with a loud expectorate of ice—or, when they did fall, how to skid rather than flail, so as not to break an ankle or bruise a tailbone. They fell relentlessly those first days, with an almost religious devotion—a cult of falling. Testing the

limits of their abilities, their feet grew to fit their skates. They graduated from racing in one heat across the ice to making toboggan-trains
that wound in tight S's, working hard to derail the caboose, to whirly-
bird, or pebble-on-a-string: a human chain, the boy in the center the
anchor, turning in rigid circles like a gear, so that the one at the end
was whipped around at speeds he couldn't attain alone. The hurdles
got taller, and more treacherous, and the boys lined up to jump them
backwards as well as forwards, the others clapping to signal the moment he should become airborne, or on one foot, mocking figure
skaters, arms out and flapping.

They invented a species of bombardment with some old tennis
balls they had found in the woods, every man for himself and every
ball up for grabs. It was an easy step from there to an anarchic hockey
without teams or goals, possession the only objective, a stone for a
puck. Any and all true pucks had disappeared the previous winter;
even a short season was enough to lose every last one, and short sea-
sons were all they had known before now, save one year without any
season at all. The pucks shot right through the snow piled by the inlet
and outlet and into the pools, they ricocheted up onto the bank or
overshot it into the trees. In the rare case that they were recovered,
they had always gone further than seemed reasonably possible. It was
weird, they should have stood out against the snow, should have been
on the banks when the snow melted in spring, waiting for them, like a
carbonized nugget of winter. They were offerings to the god of winter
for the advent of the ice. It seemed like a better explanation than the
caterpillars.

But who needed a puck? Howe, Gretzky, Messier, they might
have played with rocks growing up, too. Pele had played soccer with a
sack. And even if the stones chewed up their sticks and cut their shins
and knees through their jeans, these were just the ones they could find
within a short waddle from the ice. They looked for better ones on

the way to and from the pond: fatter than for skipping, palm-wide, vaguely round and without flinty edges. Nor was there any reason to stop with rocks. There were cans for the taking. They raided their pantries, told their parents it was for the church drive. They returned with new offerings: Alpo, Pepsi, Chef Boyardee, Fancy Feast, Green Giant, Campbell's, Chicken-of-the-Sea. The tall ones tended to roll and spin on their long axes. The soda cans burst within five minutes, spewing a syrupy slush all over the ice. The tuna and catfood cans fared better, but were too heavy to slap. They tried keying open one of the catfood cans, and smashed a soda can into a flat disk. But now they were too light, took wobbly flight on an easy pass, skipped or planed over their sticks. Stuffing a sock into the cat food can helped a little to keep it icebound. But now it dented too easily; within ten minutes it was a crumpled ball. They tried filling the tuna can with water and leaving it overnight—an ice puck with a tin housing—but the ice shattered when the puck got caught between two sticks.

For a time they toiled as dourly as men in lab coats with clipboards. A roll of electrical tape, for example, failed tests for stability (it rolled too easily) and durability (it grew more flimsy and lopsided the more they batted it around). Most plastics—jewel cases, a rolling wallpaper remover—cracked and chipped almost immediately, leaving splinters all over the ice. In the end it was a half-spent candle that came closest: it moved quickly over the ice with hardly a skitter, slightly better than a bar of soap, which took second place. It even made a mildly authentic clack when they struck it. It was only a little too light to be clearly visible—nothing a dab of paint couldn't cure—and a little too small. But when they kneaded it over fire into a wax flapjack, it lost some of its stability and traction. And whether because everything that seemed durable they managed to destroy in a matter of minutes, or because they were too young to sustain such a disciplined curiosity, they turned their energies to ludic destruction. Packages of Ramen noodles and elbow macaroni, just to watch the confetti explosions. A knot of new skate laces, the knot undoing as they dribbled it down the ice, a dead octopus. An Eggo waffle, the recoverable portions still edible. A hundred-watt lightbulb, passed as gingerly as a water balloon until somebody got up the nerve to slap it. It got to the point that, when one of them showed up with a pinewood puck he'd cut in his father's shop and spray-painted black, another ran home immediately to get a can of gasoline. They doused it, lit it, and played with it until somebody's stick caught fire, grip tape belching thick smoke like a torch. They cast it out into the woods with the rest of their failed experiments, and swept whatever remained to the edges of the ice.

After a couple of weeks one of the boys bit the bullet, collected money and convinced his father to stop at the sporting goods store on Route 6 on his way back from a job. The next day he showed up with a sackful. This much must be said for the true puck: it made such a satisfying clack when the first stick hit it that the boys actually cried out. It skittered just a little, then hugged the ice, cruised almost the length of the pond before stopping. They chased it, surrounded it. It might have been a splinter of the cross, but it looked like a hole. They built altars to it in the shape of goals. They formed themselves into teams, and since they were an odd number and never quite enough to make two full lineups, they played without goalies and one man out; he dropped the puck for face-offs, and then replaced whoever next needed to catch his breath, quickly swapping jerseys if the new man-out was on the opposing team. In this way the players on any one team changed several times throughout a scrimmage, and the play itself had no time limit beyond their collective exhaustion. Oddly, their devotion to the one team or other was the more fanatical for being so provisional. And it grew by the day, as they learned to keep their sticks down and their chins up, organized drills and ran plays of increasing violence and sophistication, practicing breakaways and three-on-twos, dumping the puck off behind them to a trailer, and stopping short with the puck trapped for a shot. They even started fights, half-serious brawls, and though they hit each other hard enough to bloody their knuckles they left the ice without grievances or apologies. It seemed like a thousand years ago they had played with stones and candles and catfood cans; they felt a foot taller, and with their new bruises and trick shots they bragged about marching down to the lake and challenging the older boys in the township league, or the community college kids who practiced at the rink down on 6, dropping a glove on the ice right in front of the penguin-high ref.

Oh, the rink. They gloated, thinking about those poor suckers. They'd all been there at one time or another, for a birthday party, or to watch a game. Crowded with idiots, loud corny music playing, ice all chewed up. Every forty minutes they had to kick everyone off and bring out the Zamboni—fun to watch, but it wasn't skating. They scrambled out as soon as they blew the horn, but got at most a couple of minutes before the ice was choked again. Everyone else was so slow. And they all went in the same direction, like they were riding a carousel, a weird procession to nowhere, pilgrims who had mistaken a circle for a line. They couldn't even imagine going the opposite way. The only remotely fun thing to do was slalom between the carousel riders. But just when they'd got up a little bit of speed, some stupid little kid would come along skating the wrong way, or they'd get stuck behind an old lady clinging to the boards like the ice was a pit of crocodiles, or one of the asshole older kids, the ones who stared at their girlfriends, would skate over in his bright yellow guard jacket and sunglasses, blowing his whistle. On the pond the boys would sometimes imitate the older kids skating over to dock them, and then flip off their effigies. The pond was three times the size of the rink. No slowpokes to run into, no corny music. No noise. No rules but the ones they made themselves.

They never did hitch that ride over to the rink to crash a scrimmage, and they never hiked the twelve miles down to the lake. All through the remainder of December and the month of January, as the temperature bobbed around freezing, dipping into the teens or lower at night, and rising into the low forties on sunnier days, they stayed at the pond. There were a few more snowfalls, none major; the boys would skate watching the dark ribbons unspool behind them, writing in a wide, looping, unintelligible cursive. When they stopped they could hear the tick of the flakes landing on the ice. Then the wind would pick up and whip the new powder into frozen waves. They would pull their hats down almost to their eyes and skate hard into it, feeling the cold bite their dry lips and wet, chapped noses, their bodies careening in their jerseys and their coats, like jibs.

They were late to everything, blinking at the world elsewhere like time travelers catapulted into the future, amazed, on reaching their destination, to find that any time had passed at all. And just as the pond stranded time, so it seemed to rewrite the geography of the valley. It lay on the line between any two points. In fact, there was no way to get anywhere but by passing it. And yet, somehow, it was not of the valley. All news from the valley dissolved into nothingness when they dropped down into the meadow on the other side of the ridge. They couldn't smell chimney smoke anymore; they couldn't hear school bells, or church bells, or the old Tilson lady, or the voices of their parents. And if they had, they would have pretended not to.

They skated before and after school and whatever time they could get away from church or chores on weekends. They got used to the clunking weight of their skates on their shoulders, which they carried with them everywhere, except into church and the classroom. They had to cut school, if only to get their chores done, and they had to shirk their chores, especially weekends, to get enough time on the ice. They even started sneaking out at night, crunching through the snow-bright woods to the pond, errant beams of their flashlights crossing on the ice, playing across the dark horizon of the snow piled on the banks and the knots of trees. When they fell, the beam of light stopped, too, a stationary cone broadcast over the ice. With the flashlights off, they were flying shadows. On clearer nights when the moon waxed near full they could see their dim shadows, and the bank was a frozen grey tide, and the trees black palisades against the blue-black sky. Silence but for the chuck and whir of their skates. They dug a pit in the clearing by the outlet and gathered kindling for a fire, the sparks flittered up to become stars, the bones in their feet were outlined in perspiration on their wet socks steaming near the fire. They brought pocketfuls of powder from shotgun shells, cast them into the fire to make it hiss and rise, like they were wizards. They brought cigarettes and beer, Skoal, pot, whiskey, a radio, magazines with pictures of cars and guns. They brought pictures of girls, sometimes with the heart-shaped scrawl of yearbook pages. They talked about girls and their teachers and their parents, about what they wanted to do or be. See the world from the deck of an aircraft carrier. Surf off Thailand, smoke grass with the hookers there. Invent something everybody wanted, make a million dollars, retire at thirty. Buy a fleet of really, really nice cars. They got to school later and later and slept what remained of the day. Why shouldn't they, when so little was expected of them there? What could what they learned there tell them about the feel of the ice and the subtle rhythms of nature? They were punished, of course, by their teachers, by their fathers. But all their teachers could do was pile on the detentions, and their fathers could think of little better than a halfhearted beating. It was rare that one thought to confiscate their skates.

One day in mid-February it started snowing while they scrimmaged. Big, wet, heavy flakes. They tried ignoring it at first, as they had before, until they could feel the slight drag of the snow against their blades, and the puck gathered a beard of snow as it dragged to a stop. The tracks made by the shovels and brooms they had left by the pond were quickly covered again behind them. They watched it snow until it had all but obscured the ice.

When they awoke the next morning there were two and a half feet on the ground. The new sun was brilliant, blinding. The snow was almost up to their hips; they moved through a frozen white surf. Trees and power lines and deer fencing and porch screens all sagged with the stuff, and the well covers and birdbaths and barn roofs were crowned with white. The mailboxes were completely buried. Along the trail they had to duck or shake off the snow-heavy branches, beating them with their shovels and sticks. When the old woman's voice rang out, it seemed to come from high above, like the cry of a hawk. Entering the hollow, the only way they could tell the pond was by the contour of the trees, and the slight depression in the snow, and the dark sockets of the inlet and outlet.

A year ago they would have been making angels and forts, piling up arsenals of snowballs. Now they dug with the sullen tenacity of men trying to tunnel their way out of prison. One boy ran home for a wheelbarrow. But it could only hold a few shovelfuls at a time, and was difficult to roll to and from the bank; the wet, heavy snow stuck to the bottom when they tried to dump it. They abandoned it on the bank, half-buried, like a beached vessel. Then somebody else got the bright idea to roll the snow out in balls, like they were building a giant snowman. But the snow refused to stick to itself. In the end they were reduced to shoveling, and shoveling, and shoveling, until, in a little more than an hour, with all hands on deck, they had managed to dig a fifteen-foot-wide trench the short way across the pond. It was fluted on either end, the white walls stood as high as full-grown corn, and with the dark ice against the snow it looked something like a UFO landing pad, just that mix of miracle and folly.

Their play was more physical than before, cramped as they were into such a small space. They were by turns giddy and frustrated, and almost too tired to hold their sticks. They left hollows up and down the snow walls, and piles of white slag on the ice; and when they couldn't play anymore for exhaustion, they occupied these hollows, like birds nesting along a rafter, skates crossed and sticks lain over their knees, and then lay back and stared up at the perfectly blue sky through the halo of snow, warm on their bellies, cold on their backs. When they were recovered they took turns speeding down the trench and somersaulting into the eight-foot-high gauntlet of snow, each boy emerging from his snow-cubby to cheers and boos and ring-announcer's prattle. The snow got up their pant legs and in their ears. By the time they left for school, betting on a late opening to save them yet another detention, they were more than usually soaked.

But a trickling had started in their ears which persisted throughout the school day, as though the water had found a way into their brains, and was rushing through the canals and crevices there. By the time they made it back to the pond that afternoon, the trench had an inch of water at the bottom. It might have been the sun reflecting off the snow, or the weight of the snow that had driven the rest of the ice sheet down, forcing the water up over it. The snow itself had packed down, and nearest the water had a blue-grey tinge, like a glacier. The boys splashed into the trench in their boots, wondering aloud if they should try to bail it. They went home flustered, ate dinner pensively, their mothers marveling at their timeliness on this of all days. They got into bed unsure whether to pray for sun or cold.

Each night as the temperature dropped, the water in the trench would freeze thinly over; and each day, as the mercury in the thermometer climbed to near fifty again, the snow would settle, feeding the reflecting-pool shaped puddle from the blue-grey layer of slush at the bottom. The boys took turns standing watch, reporting the changes to each other at school. They didn't dare raise a shovel, afraid of marring the surface, which they believed the snow would somehow keep pristine.

It took only four days for the snow to disappear from the pond. When the temperature began to drop again a couple of days later, they noticed new changes. At first the whole surface was puddled, and they were as afraid to walk on it as they had been to shovel—the boot-prints they had left at either end of the trench had already petrified into puckered craters. Soon a pane of ice half an inch thick covered the water by the bank. It cracked in long, straight lines when they tried to walk on it. Though they knew there was only an inch and a half of water between the pane and the well-frozen layer beneath, the cracking unnerved them. The ice in the place where the trench had been was smooth as glass, but ridges separated it from the rest of the pond in the places where the walls of snow had stood. Elsewhere, in the vast unshoveled territories to the north and south, the ice was a thick, fibrous white of a sort they had not seen before, and buckled nearest the banks.

Over the ensuing days the pane thickened, absorbing the inter-vening layer of water, and the boys were able to creep out onto the pond again, sliding on the rubber soles of their boots. They discovered the reason for that new, fibrous whiteness: the surface had refrozen into a white corrugate, millions of tiny cobbles that their boots skit-tered over as they slid. But their most remarkable discovery was re-served for the trench: they could see their old skatemarks through the new pane of ice and the layer of water. The ice, or the water between, or the few inches of distance the two provided, had revealed them; they looked like the vanishing patterns left behind by collisions in a particle accelerator, the same smoked-glass appearance, flecks and scatterings. All the circles and scorings of the month's meanderings were preserved there, all their individual trajectories intricately interwoven. In these lines was recorded every infinitesimally small decision they had made, whether to turn one direction or another, to speed up or slow down or stop short. Each choice was a reflection of who they were at their purest, when they were most unconsciously themselves. They had seemed so random and of the moment—and yet here they were, etched in an immutable calculus, inescapable. They were sure the answers to all their questions were here—who they were and where they were going and what the world ran on—if they could just learn to read the marks, to trace them, like a fortune teller does the lines on a palm, through their ravelings back to their beginnings, and extrapolate them out to their ends.

Skating the cobble was like riding in the bed of a pickup over a washboard road, though it was better than the moguls or the boot-shaped craters by the banks. The ridges left by the trench walls they had no choice but to jump. Their skates would scrape loudly as they carved and pedaled over the corrugate; there would be a moment of silence when they hopped the ridge into the trench; then a quiet whir-ring, until they jumped the next ridge, or turned back over the pre-vious one, their skates bumping and wobbling again, scraping when they pedaled. They had to think about where they were on the ice in a way they hadn't before, consider it strategically: how they and the puck would move differently over the cobbles than in the trench; how a skater could get clotheslined if they forgot the ridges and other pitfalls in the heat of play. Then they went down hard, the sorts of falls that made their heads jounce and teeth clack. They went down fighting, too, as though in their time off the ice they had forgotten how to fall, or had simply decided not to accept it anymore, and got up again wincing, stiff with pain, their bodies newly brittle, the ice harder than they remembered.

Over the next few days the north end of the pond started to crater and pock. From the inlet and outlet dark, coral blooms reached out under the levees of snow. The ice nearest the pools looked like the mineral terraces of a hot spring. The trickling sound had returned; they heard it in every silence. As the terrain for skating constricted yet further—though not enough yet to move the goals and play the short way across—the boys began trying to level the ridges by chiseling at them with their shovels, and breaking the crusted edges of their boot-prints off with their skates. They piled the ice pebbles with the rest of the white scrabble into the craters, hoping that a few cycles of warm days and cold nights would freeze them flat again. When this failed, they conceived an ambitious new project: cover the ice with water in the evenings, and let it freeze overnight; in a week at most it would be smooth again. They brought pails, and spent the last hour of daylight working in modified bucket brigades, one team on either end of the pond. The first boy would dunk his pail into the inlet or outlet, re-move the leaves and other debris from the freezing water before pass-ing it over to the second, who ran it a little ways around the pond to the third, who skated between the bank and the fourth, who dumped the water and underhanded the bucket back to the first. The water would wash around the fourth's boots, though on the north end only the boy filling the buckets could tell where it had pooled, and where the ice was still dry, from the way the puddles shone in the fading light. He directed the fourth like a runway worker, right and left, and then back, up to the ridge of the old trench, which served as a dam.

They were diligent for the first few days, and even got more ef-ficient as each boy fell into one of his prescribed roles. Seeing no change, they decided to station both teams on the more rapidly de-teriorating north end, where the gritty ice nearest the pool was al-ready unskateable. But as the craters continued to bloom and spread, and the terraces from the inlet reached out under the piled snow, which had itself settled into a thin scar, they were forced to recog-nize the power of the enemies ranged against them—the encroaching new season, the lengthening of the days, the sun arcing higher and higher—and to acknowledge they were fighting a losing battle. It was as though they had believed they could knock the sun down with a throw of the bucket, or snuff it with a pailful of water.

One afternoon, they spent detention idly paging through a chemistry book they had found in the classroom where they were confined. Something called a phase diagram caught their eye. Water was one of three substances illustrated. The text pointed out that the branch tilted backwards, toward the y-axis, and that for water alone this was true. Although the boys couldn't quite grasp the significance of this, they were sure it damned them in some way. If only they could have grabbed that branch and pushed it forward, like a lever, so that the diagram looked like the others. The book didn't say anything about making the branch go the other way; it just told them how things were.

Nor could the book tell them anything about why the ice pulled harder the less of it there was, like it was gaining in density what it lost in volume, a collapsing star. It was Tony's voice they heard, louder than before, and more incessant, calling them out of bed before the gloaming, into the blackest, coldest hole of night. A different dark than a month before, and a different feeling on the ice. Dour, groggy, they skated in dazed circles, like they were chained to a wheel, in unconscious parody of the rink. The games were disbanded; it already felt like a winter ago they had played. With each thrust backwards or forwards they tempted the humps and craters, trying to recall the right moments to jump or stop, at least until the morning brightened enough that they were able to see the scorings on the leaden surface. It was so cold still, colder than it had been in January, they were sure. But then the changes had nothing to do with the temperature; it was the longer days, and the angle of the sun, that kept chipping away at the ice. Every moment they spent in the classroom, or in their fathers' shops, or doing chores, or sleeping, another millimeter would have disappeared, chewed up by that devouring monster called The Sun. Or by the rain—God, the rain was even worse, every drop like a hoe, hacking away at the surface. They cut school even more, didn't even bother to report to detention, grew even more forgetful of their chores, and of the promises they made to their parents. They were told over and over to get their heads out of their asses, were threatened with groundings and expulsions, hit with belts and rods and the backs of hands. But in the whir of machinery, in the scrape of chalk against the board, they heard the old chuck and roar of the skates. And in the quiet, that trickling … it drove them back to the ice half in despair of what they would find: water, nothing. They fell asleep with the trickling sound still in their ears, bruised and tired and barely an hour after dinner, blue light on the horizon and the moon yet to rise, dreamt of skating in absolute darkness on a pond whose banks receded to infinity. They woke in the dark to the sound of trickling, like to an alarm.

The whole world was melting. The water rushing under the sewer grates drowned out the sounds of their footsteps on the gravel road, ran with a fury that threatened to wash the whole town out the end of the valley. The wet made the land seem to burn with an interior light. Boulders glowed black, and in places the moss had turned the ground an electric green. The shallow ravines all ran like the sewers over exposed leaf rot, and icicles dripped from every rocky overhang, as they did from the eaves of their houses and barns. The snow was peppered all over with the wriggling larvae of some insect just being born, a hundred in every bootprint. Even tulips and crocuses had started to push up through the packed-down snow. Soon the trees and fields would swarm with phoebes and blackbirds and yellowthroats, their voices almost as incessant as the trickle; the first slow wasps would appear drunk with cold, the first geese would leave their snaking green dung on the grass. The boys would have to elbow their way through the spiderwebs grown between trees. And they would, un-thinkingly, splashing through the puddled gullies, crunching over the larva-strewn snow. Not even that haunting ululation could call them back to themselves. They would pause at the stream, all thawed now, fast and a little swollen, and think about the changes happening all around them, the changes they had noticed in their own homes—the cats taken to sunning themselves outside the doors of barns, the tiny newborn spiders depending from light fixtures and showerheads and bannisters, the ladybugs come out of hibernation to congregate in the upstairs windows, fanning out into the light. They would skitter by, shadows on the paint; their bodies would tick against the glass, snow on ice, snow on ice … the boys would look up to see them slow-ly folding their wings back under their colored shells. Watching the strong current of the stream, they thought about all these things, but refused to mention them, as if not doing so was a way to not acknowl-edge them to themselves. Sometimes it even flurried a little while they stood there, like the winter was teasing them with coming back.

There was a last hard snowfall in early March, almost a foot. Walking across the pond, they left grey, watery prints. It was unclear quite what they were walking on, where the snow became slush, and slush ice; there seemed to be no firm boundary anymore, nothing stopping them from sinking all the way down. After rain had melted the last of the snow on the pond, the whole surface turned grey and porous. They brought out the shovels again, pushing the slush in even rows and piling it by the banks, muddy now, almost impassable. But with every pass of the shovel there was more wet ice to push. The surface remained porous, and their boots left faintly-visible imperfec-tions behind them, no matter how softly they stepped, or how care-fully they tried to lave the surface even.

When the temperature dropped again, the south end froze into a brittle-looking, pale mass, covered with fungal abscesses, and mottled with puddles in the afternoons. Elsewhere the ice remained in steady retreat, pulling away from the banks like a herd of ungulates huddling from wolves. The pool by the inlet had grown into a wide sickle of water, and its thorny fingers reached yet further underneath the terraced ledge where the ice sheet began, almost to where the trench had been, whose traces had disappeared in the last snow. It was clear the sheet was floating now, like an ice cube in a glass of water, riding low. In the places where the bank had managed to refreeze, the ice looked flimsy, like the skin on a pot of scalding milk, so different from the first glassy panes they had gleefully broken back in early December. They could only get onto the sheet from a few places along the southeast bank, which was comparatively unchanged. If it had snowed the previous night, they trekked joined at the wrists to the place where it had stuck, until their feet began to slide; then they dropped down onto the cobbled ice and changed into their skates, the wet soaking them through their jeans, and carved in grim little circles, like prisoners in an exercise yard, eyes closed to the too-early sun, birds mocking them from the trees. Most afternoons they didn't even try, though they still came out and sat amid the grainy hillocks of snow that remained of the heaps they had shoveled, smoking and cussing and squinting at the puddles, wondering how long they had left. Sometimes they believed it was only their loyalty that had kept it here this long. And yet each time they walked out onto the sheet, they swore they could feel it shrinking, curling back at its edges, forcing them to skate in smaller and smaller circles, spiraling inwards. Every day it grew more fragile, and brittle, and transparent—and they with it, as though they, too, were melting at their cores, withdrawing at their edges. One day, their teachers would turn around and find nothing but a puddle of water under their desks; one morning, their mothers would come into their rooms to find the sheets soaked through, but no other sign that a boy had been there at all.

Early one morning in mid-March they came upon a pair of ducks floating in the sickle by the inlet, parsing their lives with the quiet prepossession of horses. Seeing the boys approach, they fled into the slush, half-paddling, half-waddling, unable quite to do either, so that they moved hobbledly, bodies jerking up and down. They wound apart and together, cleaving a broken, zipper-like trail. The boys crept after them, squatting now and again to observe their labored movements—until one got too close, or the ducks spotted the invisible rifle he raised, or heard the bullet sound he made with his lips. Then they leapt up with a wattle and cry and thrum of the wings, flapped away over the nearest trees, leaving that meandering track in the slush to dead-end in a mysterious blank, where all signs of the trail-maker vanished.

It was maybe five minutes later that the leading boy went down all the way to his hips. It happened so quickly he didn't have time to cry out, and he almost dragged the rest down with him. As it was, the last couple hadn't even stepped off the bank yet—though they had to, once the first was safely out of the water, his pants and the skirts of his jersey all dark. Heaving, his skates still slung over his shoulder, he was rambling quietly about feeling something tugging on his legs. They took turns shuffling as close as they dared to the edge of the hole, each announcing what he saw or didn't see, except the last, who knelt down and put his hand in the pool, so that the water rippled gently.

They saw the old Tilson lady's cat on the way home. They did. White, with a black patch under its chin. Crossing twenty yards ahead of them, it looked once in their direction, one hoary paw raised, eyes slits of yellow marble, and then continued on through the brush in the direction of the old lady's house. They did not hear her calling.

*

They gave Bill's dad a promotion and moved him to Vermont. He manages a new store there, a crew of fifteen, Bill helps out on the floor. Jake's parents split up, he moved with his mom downstate, closer to her family. Dan shacked up with Erica and had a kid, every time you see him he's rushing from one thing to another, talking about pulling down OT, though if you can hold onto him for five minutes it's clear he's between jobs again. Timmy went on to college. They said he shouldn't have gone so far, and when he flunked out after his first year, that he should have come back. Joey ended up in prison after he and some of his new buddies at the Shell station down on 6 started making meth. He was never too careful. They put his face on posters, not that you'd recognize him. Cal, he got work as a guard. Different facility—there's so many you wouldn't think there were enough boys to fill them, but there are. They send most of them from downstate. Kevin and Edison joined up, like they always said they would, got shipped off to Afghanistan. Kevin did two tours, came home to a bunch of people waving little flags at the airport. He walks around a lot at night. The rest—Hal, Zach, Chase—would have followed their dads to the gas fields. But since they finally developed Clausen and Everton properties, they didn't have to go anywhere. The tankers roll right down Main now; the old men stand around and wave. The Tilson pond goes on freezing and thawing, freezing and thawing, and every year it freezes a little less thick, and thaws a few days earlier, and the winters get shorter and shorter as the days get longer.

THE POND

MY WIFE AND I HAVE A SMALL POND ON OUR PROPERTY. IT'S SHAPED like a kidney, and fed by a spring, and stocked with three different kinds of fish. The fish eat the bugs, and each other; the spring helps to keep the surface relatively scumless. A muskrat lives in our pond, too. On some mornings I wait for its brown head to break the surface of the water, cruise the length of the pond, and then disappear. The first time I saw it, I mistook it for an otter. There is a willow tree on the bank opposite the house, and a stubby grey dock on the near one. A boat, the same color as the dock, lies perennially overturned in the tall grass.

It was for the pond, not the house, that we bought the property. We imagined a future of morning coffees on the dock, or on lawn chairs set out on the far bank under the willow, and, when we weren't lost in each other's eyes, staring down into the calm, relatively scumless water, and sighing wistfully. We imagined ourselves floating the long hot summer days away in the boat, sipping cocktails, and drawing up tiny, shimmering fish on a string.

But once we stopped looking at each other, we lost interest in the pond as well. The pond became something to be thankful for because it didn't need to be mowed, and required only minimal upkeep—unlike the century-old house, which seemed to be falling to pieces around us. In time we came to resent the pond—resent it for its serene, unchanging beauty, unmindful of us, while the lawn went to weeds, and the house crumbled, and our marriage beached itself on a bored lethargy, punctuated by sudden, violent arguments over the pettiest things.

Not that we ever abused each other physically. But objects had a tendency to get broken. Glasses and windows shattered, shirts torn to rags, slippers thrown in the fire, random appliances vandalized. Once, when she locked me out of the house, I kicked in the front door. She was standing right on the other side with her arms crossed, said, "Are you proud of yourself?" Once, she went into my closet and peed on my shoes, though she was drunk at the time and still claims not to remember. That was when I broke her mixer—ran it until the motor coughed smoke. It had a lifetime warranty.

We called this sort of thing our marriage penalty: the price we paid in consumer goods and other forms of property to maintain the trappings of a stable relationship.

One summer day, while we were arguing about something—I've never managed to remember what—my wife got up off her recliner, went into the bedroom, and came back with my bowling ball. She stood there holding it in both hands, like she was unsure what to do with it. Such a big, smooth, heavy ball, marbled purple. An opportunity not to be wasted. I was waiting for it to go through a window. I even wondered, fleetingly, if she was going to drop it on my foot, or my head. But she walked right past me, pushed her way through the screen door.

I had another vision, this time of the ball going through the windshield of the car.

Then I heard a boom-splash, like the sound of someone doing a cannonball off the high dive at the pool. When I made it to the window, she was standing on the end of the dock, wiping her hands together theatrically.

"You fucking bitch," I said.

I watched her make her way back to the house, swinging her arms. The screen door slammed behind her; she fell heavily back into her recliner.

Then she asked me, sweetly, to make her a gin and tonic.

Instead, I went into the bedroom. My empty bowling bag sat on the end of the bed, zipper undone. I wasn't much of a bowler anymore—once a month if I was lucky—so I don't know why I was trembling. I was thinking, I can do the same goddamn thing to *her* ball. But that would have just made us even. Even was never the point. The point was to escalate.

I went into her closet and took out everything I could carry, grabbing hangers in sets of three and four and draping her blouses and dresses and suits over my arm. When they were piled so high I could barely see over the top, I stumbled back into the den, almost tripping on the hassock on my way to the door. I heard her shriek, and then she was pawing at me, calling me an asshole. She managed to grab away a few dresses before I could hug the pile against my chest and, swinging my shoulders, bully my way outside. For some twisted reason, I got this image of carrying her across the threshold the day we were married.

It was a warm night. A fish or two broke the surface of the pond as I half-staggered, half-ran through the tall grass, the clothes flapping. At the end of the dock I opened up my arms, the way a child will drop a bunch of leaves. The stack fell all in a clump into the water, started floating away, spinning slowly in the invisible current. A few pieces separated, mapping other swirls and eddies. I went and got a stick and started to push the air out of the near ones, pitched stones at the ones I couldn't reach. What I wouldn't have given to see her wedding dress floating around in there, like a big white lily pad.

I was just going inside when she came out with an armload of books. Not just any books: volumes of the *Encyclopedia of World History* that had belonged to my father.

The gloves are off, I thought. But I resisted the urge to tackle her. In fact, I held the door open, watched her hump those heavy books all the way to the pond, my heart sinking with each step. Not that I had read any of them. But I was always intending to, and somehow that made it worse.

She didn't bother with the dock. Instead, she dropped the armload by the bank, and then started casting them in one at a time, holding the volumes by their corners and turning circles with her body to gather momentum. She grunted as each one left her hands, and took a few seconds between throws to watch the ripples spread.

Now I toured my own house like it was a rummage sale, listening for the last few grunts-and-splashes from the pond. The dishes; there were some she really valued, though I couldn't remember which, or why. Gifts, some of them. Better to err on the side of caution. I made a stack of as many as I could carry, treated them like she had my father's encyclopedias, frisbeeing them from the end of the dock one at a time, in her direction, though well short of the bank.

She just stood there watching me, still and silent as a manor ghost. Behind her loomed our little blue monument to domesticity, all open to the night, windows and doors lighted. The moon had risen, though only half of it showed. I closed my eyes for a moment, listening to the frogs. When I opened them again, she had gone running back toward the house. I knew what she was feeling, that impulse to find something else to drown.

There were still a couple of dishes left when she came staggering back outside, a garbage bag slung over her shoulder. She weaved her way through the grass and right up onto the dock, stopped just a few feet short of me, dropped the bag, pushed it over, and shook its contents out over the side. It was full of clothes, a few pairs of shoes thrown in. I recognized the shoes, or some of them—the ones that floated.

I handed her my stick, and we stood there watching the clothes of mine she could not sink drift in the same direction hers had, toward the reeds, where some of hers I hadn't been able to sink had gotten stuck. Listening to her breath heave and settle, I thought we might be on the point of calling a truce. I felt her eyes on me, but when I looked at her she was staring at the water again, the stick still in her hands. I couldn't parse her expression: sadness and longing, rage, malicious humor, all mixed together.

She pitched the stick into the grass and started back toward the house; and I realized that, whatever I believed I had seen in her expression, it wasn't conciliation.

We were just getting started.

We spent the next few hours ransacking the house, rushing around like evacuees, sometimes in the same room, sometimes in different ones. I would hear drawers pulled out, their contents emptied onto sheets staked out like tarps, the sheets tied into bundles, the bundles carried to the pond. Her stuff, my stuff—it stopped mattering: it was all just *stuff*, and it all had to go. And there was so much of it, much more than I would ever have believed we had. Photo albums, decorative lamps, vinyl, books, more books, all but a few titles unfamiliar. Framed posters for art exhibits bought in some museum gift shop. A lacquered conch shell from some ancient Caribbean vacation. The small cross that hung over our bed, the music box on the mantle—"Für Elyse," I think; I didn't open it. The pistol, mine, a Glock, last used to shoot at fish one drunken evening. The archery set, hers. From the garage, the sawdust pillow targets, and the bikes, rolled right off the bank. Every species of tool, and the wheelbarrow to carry them, and then follow them into the water. Stacks of fabric, batting for quilts. The sewing machine, heavy as an alternator, cord dragging. From the attic, old hockey gear, cobwebbed dumbbells, a fishing pole and tackle box, a plastic rocking horse on wheels. Some of it I didn't even know we still had, or had given up on finding. If I found it myself, I'd bark out a laugh, stop just short of calling her. Not that I saved anything. At least now I would know where to find it.

When we got to the larger things—the recliners, the black leather loveseat, the thirty-nine-inch flatscreen TV—we could no longer afford to pass each other without looking or speaking. It would require a minimal amount of cooperation to carry what we could between us, and drag what we couldn't. And so we did, first with the TV: a terrific splash when it hit the water, it bobbed once and sank like a stone. The loveseat took longer, but when at last it sank, it went down like a tanker, at a forty-five-degree angle, one end standing out entirely from the surface, and then sliding slowly under, the water around it hissing. We both waved as we watched it disappear. Our eyes met, briefly. We were smiling.

She said, "Now let's throw in the fucking bed."

We took it in three parts: mattress, box spring, and frame. We couldn't stop laughing the whole time. At one point, while we were carrying the mattress, I said, "The conjugal bed," in this deep, radio-announcer's voice, and she lost it so bad she dropped her end. I dropped mine, too. The mattress flopped over, and we sat on it until we had recovered ourselves enough to carry it the rest of the way.

We reassembled the bed on the dock, didn't even bother to strip the sheets, just flipped the whole contraption right into the water. Maybe going in upside-down, with the metal frame on top, the empty chamber of the box spring flooding, helped it sink, because it went down like the TV: one quick bob and it was gone.

By then we had dumped so much stuff into the pond that I kept waiting for something to poke through. It wasn't a big pond—surely it wasn't big enough to hold the joint rubble of our miserable lives. But apart from the few things that floated, all of which we diligently tried to sink, the pond swallowed everything we threw at it.

When the house had grown bare as an abandoned museum, we sat down at the end of the dock, our legs dangling. A fit of laughter when she mentioned the piano we did not own; images of it sending up jets of water, like a drowning leviathan—and then, when it was entirely submerged, sinking silently, like an astronaut falling through space. Another fit when I suggested we drive the car in. I didn't have the energy to, and I guess she didn't, either. Anyway, I was pretty sure the keys were already at the bottom. The clothes on our backs were the last things to go. We watched them float away like clouds. Then from the night-church in the reeds the frogs rose up in a guttural plainchant, and a number of fish broke the surface almost in unison, as though we had made them an offering. We made love for the first time in longer than I could remember, there on the dock, under the half-moon, for an audience of a few thousand visible stars. Then we fell asleep.

A trace of that moon still hung on the horizon the next morning, or we might have believed everything had been made new. Earth like the shell of a robin's egg. Sunlight falling dappled through leaves. Pond glowing like molten silver. We awoke stunned, and a little ashamed. Unable quite to look at each other, we turned our gaze on the pond. And imagine our surprise when, peering down beyond our reflections, past the meandering fish, all the way to the bottom, we found that our belongings had sunk, if not into the positions they had originally occupied, then into a passable reflection of domesticity. The bed had somehow righted itself, sheets swaying like weeds; the loveseat had settled a few feet away from the sunken TV, which was turned to face it. Even the clothes had clumped together in a closet-like drift.

It was more than passable; it was beautiful. And the longer we looked, the more beautiful it became. It was like one of those miniature castles you put in the bottom of a fish tank, near the bubbling filter, so that the goldfish have something to swim through. We recognized our life together, staring back at us from beneath the water, beyond the shadows of ourselves. And when we could no longer abide just looking, we threw ourselves in.

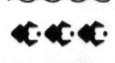

CARLS

MY HUSBAND AND I HAVE TWO NEIGHBORS NAMED CARL. ONE CARL lives in the house next to the house next to ours. The other lives seven houses away in the opposite direction, on the other side of the street. The nearer Carl—furtive Carl—bikes around the neighborhood on an old Schwinn five-speed with an orange flag clipped to the seat. We'll hear him coming before we see him, because he likes to ring his bell, as if to say, *Carl's here!* He seems to ring it whenever it suits him; we're never sure if he deliberately rings in front of some people's houses, but not others', and if so, what it means.

This bike-riding and bell-ringing would be tolerable enough if furtive Carl didn't fire up his excavator in the middle of the night to perform some ambiguous labor in his backyard.

We never see furtive Carl outside his house except on his bike—never see more than the elbow of his excavator over the fence a house away. Gregarious Carl, on the other hand, spends entire days in his front yard, wearing nothing but Bogs and longjohns, hacking away with trowel or hoe. His work seems to involve the endless, tormented carting of wheelbarrows full of earth between one part of the yard and another. As he grunts and sweats, he caterwauls away to the opera that blares from speakers pushed up against his window screens. If anyone passes by, he calls out, loudly enough that he can be heard over the music, and waves his arms over his head, as if to fend off a buzzard that had mistaken him for carrion.

My husband says the opera is Wagner. Perhaps gregarious Carl is German? We've never gotten close enough to ask. He is very pale, despite the long days spent toiling shirtless in the sun. Furtive Carl's ethnicity is similarly mysterious. Some of our neighbors believe he is Korean, though they have never explained why.

The Carls are widely regarded as harmless lunatics, with some believing that gregarious Carl should be labeled mentally deficient, rather than simply foreign. But are the Carls really harmless? Consider the matter of our property values. No one likes to live in the vicinity of weirdos. Consider our quality of life: the peace and security, C-plus schools, and extremely low taxes which were all factors in our decision to move here. Even as we do our best to dance around the subject of the Carls in our daily intercourse over our neighbors' fences, and across the six-foot strips of grass between our perfectly-flat driveways, and from the windows of our adjacent automobiles, commenting on the unseasonable warmth, the performance of our high school varsity teams (go Hedgehogs!), or the fee increase for picking up our carefully-sorted recycling, we recognize the tell-tale weariness around our neighbors' eyes, and the way the corners of their mouths pull down, from looking at our own faces in the mirror.

At the same time, the Carls have created in us a certain wariness about how we are perceived: everyone fears that their neighbors will begin to regard them as Carls, even when their name is not Carl. No one wants to be responsible for the Carlification of their neighborhood, whatever their name happens to be.

At this point it probably bears mentioning that we have a son named Carl. Of course, we named him Carl before moving here, which is to say, before we lived near a couple of freaks named Carl, or maybe better, before we knew that other people named Carl, who happen to be freaks, were our neighbors.

For quite some time after we moved, we didn't know whether our neighbors Carl knew that we had a son named Carl. We suspected not, and we did everything in our power to keep it that way. We did so by forbidding, or at least strongly discouraging, forbidding never getting very far with teenagers—more often than not it backfires—Carl (our son) from approaching the Carls (our neighbors), and cautioning him to avoid either Carl's house. But with a Carl in either direction, and no other outlet, the injunction had no real force, since observing it would have made it impossible for Carl (our son) to go anywhere by himself, which, like any normal teenage boy, he onanistically craved, and which, after all, was one of the reasons we chose to buy in this neighborhood.

He might, in other words, take the long way around, to avoid gregarious Carl (whose house, though further away from ours, is closer to the nearest cross-street), only to run into furtive Carl. Or vice-versa. As such, the best we could do was to advise Carl (our son) not to stop when passing Carls' (our neighbors') houses; that if anyone should call out to him—anyone, that is, named Carl—he should pretend not to hear; and that, since we were afraid his bicycle would create a pretext for furtive Carl to strike up a conversation—this even as we understood that Carl's expensive mountain bike, with its two-dozen gears, preposterously large shock absorbers, and super-lightweight frame meant for hikers to carry up waterfalls and over craggy peaks, would more likely intimidate furtive Carl than interest him; that, in fact, the opposite was more likely to happen, Carl (our son) being much the less furtive of the two—he should prefer bicycle to foot when passing gregarious Carl's house, and consider pedaling more quickly, while, if he had to pass furtive Carl's house, he should prefer to walk, or rather run. These were only recommendations, of course; Carl is his own person. But they were offered in good faith.

Not surprisingly, our offers to drop him at the nearest corner, beyond where any Carl could see (barring, of course, the appearance of furtive Carl on his bike), and our invitations to text us a pick-up time and location, were rebuffed. A typical exchange:

Carl: "I'm going over to Matt's house."

Us: "We'll drop you off on Greenbriar."

Carl: "No, that's okay."

Us: "Remember to keep walking. Don't stop, whatever you do."

Carl: "I'm taking my bike."

Us: "Not past furtive Carl's!"

Carl: "Which one is that again?"

Matt is Carl's friend from school. Obviously.

The only other solution would have been to advise Carl to cut through our neighbors' properties—the very normal neighbors in whose good graces we longed to remain, both for our own standing and for the health of our community. Besides, everyone has a fence around their property, even the Carls. One of our neighbors, an elderly widow, glued broken glass along the top rail of her fence. To keep the cats out, she said; the cats eat her songbirds. At first I thought she said Carls, not cats. I am aware they sound nothing alike.

I mentioned the lack of an outlet, so I should probably clarify that, even though our street is named Pine Tree Circle, it's less a circle than a straight line, and has no pine trees that we're aware of, though it might have at one time, before we moved here, say, or before the woods were cleared.

One further clarification. I said "we have a son named Carl"; I probably should have said "our son is named Carl," since we have only one son. Even this statement is not entirely free of ambiguity, since it doesn't rule out the possibility that Carl has sisters, who may or may not be named Carl. It would be unusual, true, if less so than, say, twenty years ago, but you would still probably be safe to assume that we have only one child named Carl, as a sister would more likely be named Carla, or Carly, or Carlotta, or Karla, with a K, though the K doesn't really help matters, unlike spelling Jerry with a G, say, which helps, a little. There is in fact nothing unusual about the spelling of Carl's name, my husband and I made certain of this, it is quite standard, unlike mine, which has an extra consonant and an unorthodox vowel replacement. A celebrity whose autograph I asked for once told me that the spelling of my name was "wild."

You might also opine that it would be strange to have more than one child with the same first name, not to mention confusing, and you might be right, if a little judgmental—uncommon might be preferable; but your conviction might buckle in the face of champion pugilist George Foreman, who called all his five sons George, and then gave each a number, as though they had descended from each other, rather than belonging to the same generation. He even named his popular grill George. And while you might consider this an extreme case, and narcissistic to boot, or simply a product of the brain damage often associated with middle-aged boxers, bear in mind that Mr. Foreman is a celebrity, just like the one who said the spelling of my name is wild. No one had ever said that to me before, the most I ever got was unusual. But after that I spent a lot of time looking over the spelling of my name, and it came to seem less and less like a sixth finger, and

I decided against normalizing it, which I had once planned on doing when I grew up. Of course, my neighbors don't know how my name is spelled, since it's pronounced the same as when it is spelled normally. Anyway, you must know that celebrities make up their names, sometimes their celebrity names are completely unrelated to their given names, and other times they shorten them, to make them sound less foreign, and so easier to pronounce and remember.

By the way, where was Mrs. Foreman in all of this? Did she give her consent to becoming a George-making factory? It's like the boys were all cloned from him, and she was no more than an incubator. I can't help but see them as a graduated series of bald, avuncular little boxers, like disassembled nesting dolls; or like the transformation sequence in a fifties science-fiction movie, where an otherwise-normal animal grows monstrously large due to radioactive fallout.

But I see I have digressed.

For quite a while after we first discovered the existence of the Carls, we were fairly certain they did not know each other. At the same time, we recognized that such an encounter was inevitable, that we could do no more than brace ourselves for the consequences via a sort of mental and social sandbagging. Before long, we knew that furtive Carl would come along ringing his bell; gregarious Carl, catching sight of him, would blurt something like Achtung! so loud it almost knocked furtive Carl off his bike; furtive Carl, who in most such circumstances only pedaled faster, would stop and walk his bike up gregarious Carl's dirt-strewn driveway; and before they even knew each other's names, they would recognize an indescribable affinity.

And so it happened that one day we saw gregarious Carl, who we had never seen outside his yard, loping toward furtive Carl's house, a slantways, Bogs-heavy walk, as though one of his legs was fake, humming as he went. The following day, we heard furtive Carl ride by ringing his bell furiously in anticipation of seeing gregarious Carl.

We knew then that a pact had been sealed, a chain reaction begun, a countdown to reach minimum safe distance initiated.

Our chief concern was for Carl, our Carl, who had watched the whole debacle unfold from his bedroom window. We considered installing locking shutters. We invited him to switch to the spare bedroom, which looked out on the backyard; we dropped little hints, like, *It's amazing the way that room stays cool year-round, isn't it?* and, *Don't you think that life-size poster of Johannes Kepler would look even more awesome on the pitched ceiling of the spare room?*

Carl rolled his eyes, reminded us again that it was Nicolaus Copernicus, not Kepler. Why couldn't we keep them straight?

We knew that, when Carl went outside, the Carls united would be that much harder to avoid. Our house had been reduced to nothing more than a milepost along the highway of their weirdness. Once again we pledged to forestall the encounter for as long as we could. We made every effort to time Carl's departures to the movements of the Carls, e.g., if we saw gregarious Carl loping toward furtive Carl's house, that would mean the coast was clear in one direction, and Carl would be green-lighted to leave, once he had sworn to go the proper way. One of us would then shepherd Carl out the door, while the other kept lookout from behind the curtains. A Thumper-like tap-tap-tap on the glass would alert the other to a Carl's approach, and the shepherd would attempt to distract Carl with a feigned health emergency, or gushing exclamations about the flora on a neighbor's lawn, or some glory in the suburban sky.

Unfortunately, the Carls' movements fit no discernable pattern, such as "furtive Carl bikes toward gregarious Carl's house on Thursday evenings," or, "Gregarious Carl lopes toward furtive Carl's on Saturday mornings." Furtive Carl was the real wild card: we never knew when his bike might appear over the nearest speed hump, the menace of his bell sounding in the distance. Vegetation on the surrounding lawns was too scant for cover, and there were as yet no trees mature enough to hide behind.

We invented new chores. We grounded Carl for the most minor infractions. We planned family outings to local cultural and historical sites that none of us had ever had the slightest interest in visiting. Weekends were a real game of cat and mouse, and I'm afraid Carl often got the better of us. But the most dangerous time was the couple of hours after school, before my husband got home from work, when creative vigilance was left entirely up to me. The Carls tended to be active at this hour, too, as much as they tended be anything. For a time I tried to mirror their unpredictability—picking Carl up from school, say, and then announcing that we were all going for ice cream, inviting his friends. But while his friends were by and large enthusiastic, Carl only grew more sullen, and suspicious, until he, too, became unpredictable, and even crafty about his movements—disabling the backdoor alarm, and never leaving school through the same exit.

Then one day Carl came home with an orange flag affixed to the seat of his bike. At first we thought he had borrowed furtive Carl's bike. But furtive Carl's bike, as I think I've already made clear, was a banana-seated throwback to the sorts of bikes my husband and I rode growing up. There was a certain felicity between such a bike and a flag. The incongruity between Carl's rugged, reasonably-expensive mountain bike and that bright orange flag struck us as simply absurd.

I should add that, if Carl's bike seems a bit excessive for our development, whose streets are exceedingly flat, it was in no way out of keeping with the sorts of bikes Carl's friends rode—in fact, this was one of our primary motivations for buying him a new bike after we moved. Nothing filled our hearts with greater joy than to see Carl lined up with the other neighborhood kids, to watch him pedal furiously and catch air over a speed hump. And yet at some point I began to feel misgivings; I came almost to pity him, and all the neighborhood kids with him. Even the sidewalks were devoid of the exciting unevenness of the typical sidewalk in the older communities where my husband and I grew up. There, the roots of old trees and the cycles of freeze and thaw had raised and driven apart the paving stones like continental plates.

Was I the only parent who felt this way?

My husband and I were out tidying up the yard, the day we heard the bell and looked up to see Carl, ringing furiously as he pedaled toward a speed hump. Furtive Carl materialized a half-block further down. Then gregarious Carl came loping from the other direction to meet them, waving his arms contentedly.

The scene we had so long dreaded coalesced before our eyes. As the mounted Carls eddied around him, gregarious Carl began holding forth about something in his window-rattling baritone. Even this close, we couldn't understand a word he said.

That night in bed, my husband and I held each other for almost a quarter of an hour. It had been some time.

The next day we called a family meeting. We forbade Carl from seeing the Carls, knowing how little good this could do, particularly now that the circuit had been closed. My husband made a series of snide remarks about the orange flag. He asked Carl how he could ever expect to grow up to be a man, to take his rightful place in society, make a contribution, sire a family, if he rode around practically bedecked in orange like a crossing guard, and ringing his bell like an ice-cream vendor.

Through it all Carl said not a word, just watched us like we were some particularly loathsome species of alien, with tentacles, or pincers, or pedipalps.

It was worse; for, in the moments of silence between our exasperated interrogations and harangues, Carl hummed quietly to himself, as though his mind were entirely elsewhere, wrapped around an elusive melody beamed to him through the cosmos.

"Carl!" I shouted. "What do you see in these people? What do they offer you that your father and I don't?"

He stared like he didn't understand the question. Shrugged.

"We just hang out," he said.

Later I asked my husband whether he'd heard the humming.

"Wagner," he said. "It's goddamn *Wagner*."

I waited.

"I recognized it from Carl's stereo. Didn't you?"

Predictably enough, Carl's friends began to take an interest in the Carls as well. Soon, we were sure, Carl's friends' parents would see Carl as the rotten apple that had spoiled a perfectly good batch. The blame for their sons' downfalls would then spread to us. We, too, would become Carls.

They were a posse, with their orange flags and their bells that whirred like cicadas. Something about the way the sound reverberated between our tightly-packed houses made our blood freeze. They were like Vikings, bellowing into their shields as they entered combat. And beneath it all, the distant rumble of Wagner, the siren-song they rode toward, as toward an immolation, furtive Carl leading the way, gregarious Carl loping up the rear.

We refused to be cowed; we were, after all, the authority figures. We descended to the street to intercept them. But when we arrived, we found the Carls themselves had disappeared. The boys had all stopped, straddling their bikes, their thumbs poised on their bells. They stared at us in the new quiet with an eerie focus, almost feral. That terse friendship of teenage boys, where everything is blood-pact, and little need be spoken. We wheeled around looking for Carl, our Carl, in the crowd. But we could no longer tell which was son and which was neighbor; every boy was indistinguishable from every other. We dreaded to call his name, only to receive a chorus of replies.

One afternoon I went into the garage on some garden errand and was surprised to find Carl's bike there, sitting quietly, its front wheel cocked like a ballerina's foot, orange flag hanging limp in the gloom. I straddled it, and then slowly eased myself down onto the seat. It was firmer than I expected. Suddenly, I remembered the way my haunches would hurt after a day of riding. I remembered the hills of my old neighborhood, the way we would walk our bikes up them and then ride down, over and over. I remembered the feeling of the wind in my hair, and how my mother would complain when she tried to get the brush through it. I remembered skidding out and scraping my elbow and knee on the gravelly road, and wincing as my mother scrubbed pebbles and dirt out of the wound. The marvelous smell of A&D ointment. I remembered all these things, like Carl's bike was Don Quixote's wooden horse.

I opened my eyes again and looked down at the bell. Had I had a bell like this on my bike? I must have.

So why couldn't I remember?

I rang it, and was so startled by the noise that I quickly cupped my hand over it. In the sudden silence I could just hear the traces of reverberation off the concrete walls and cans of turpentine.

Days would go by without either of us knowing where Carl was, or what he was doing. It's not as though he was sneaking around; he didn't even bother to disarm the backdoor alarm anymore. If I heard the three beeps, I didn't get up to see if it was Carl, or whether he was entering or leaving. My husband turned up the volume on the TV. For all we knew it could have been a burglar. The next morning I'd find muddy shoeprints leading from the backdoor to Carl's room. I'd throw open his door, expecting to find them sitting together on Carl's bed, truants all. But the most incriminating thing I ever found was an open window. After a while I stopped bothering to close it; it would just be open again the next day.

I considered asking my husband to call another family meeting, the two of us confronting Carl again, demanding to know where he went, what he did. As if, when I leaned my head against the warm glass of his window, the cool air rising up through the vent at my feet, I didn't see the tracks left by the excavator. As if, lying in bed at night, I didn't hear the snorting motor, and the whirring bells cheering it on, the miasma of opera undergirding it all, like the dark against which a wilderness of stars once appeared. As if I hadn't gone to the window and watched it roll by, the boys all following it like a parade float, each with his flag and bell, and then convinced myself the next morning it had been a dream. As if I hadn't seen the lights come on in the upstairs windows of the surrounding houses, the silhouettes of neighbors tying on their robes, their heads haloed as they pressed their faces up to the glass.

There were days I dragged the hose down the driveway and sprayed off the street. I liked watching the muddy water burble along the curbstones. But I never did more than make a few puddles for mosquitoes to breed in. I could no longer tell the beep of the reversing excavator from the beep of the backdoor alarm, or the beep of the microwave Carl used to heat up his frozen burritos. Night sounded closer with the windows cracked, the neighborhood cinched up, the fences torn down. The houses were just as defenseless: the excavator's palsied mechanical arm would start digging into one side, clawing away at the wound it had made, like an infection. Before you knew it, the whole structure would collapse.

The lawn took on a few extra inches of grass; the house looked like it had grown a beard. On my way to get the mail, I tripped over a hole the size of a groundhog's burrow. There were three others, all about the same size, their edges level, the dirt carted away. I still hadn't hazarded to take Carl's bike out of the garage—it was always there now—though I spent long afternoons mounted on it, sweltering. I fantasized about my husband coming home early from work and finding me here. He would open the garage door and stand for a moment in gunfighter silhouette, before bending me over Carl's bike and taking me in full view of the neighborhood.

But when at last he did find me, he came through the side door. His eyes were bloodshot, his face haggard.

He said, "What happened to your hair?"

I didn't know what he meant, but I asked him if he liked it.

That night, I woke up to find the bed empty beside me. The bathroom light was off. I crept into the family room, where I found my husband in his pajamas sitting on one of the ottomans we used with the recliners. He had scooted it up next to the stereo, his head was bowed close to a speaker. I could just make out the strains of the melody we had heard Carl humming at our first and last family meeting.

It was almost dawn when he came back to bed. I feigned sleep. When his breath grew regular, I went down to the kitchen and took the pad I used to make shopping lists off the refrigerator. I didn't know what I intended to write. Maybe nothing, because I ended up writing my name, just my name, over and over, on those lines meant for food items. When I had covered the page, I tore if off and stuck it to the fridge with a magnet, as though it were a note saying where I was going. Then I took Carl's bike and started to ride.

The sun was just up. The flat streets steamed slightly. Birds hopped on the lawns, chirping. I rang the bell, not caring anymore if anyone heard me, if anyone saw me. No one but me, I said to myself, over and over, no one but me. It sounded so pleasant in the fresh morning air. The orange flag nodded and fluttered over my head; I could just see it when I tossed my head back, or looked over my shoulder. Wind tousled my hair to the point that no brush could ever get through. I rode all the way to the end of Pine Tree Circle, which is not a circle, and does not have any pines.

GRAVEYARD

I LIVE ACROSS THE STREET FROM A GRAVEYARD, WHICH SITS ON A hillside. My bedroom is on the second story of my little house, at the level of some of the more distant graves. Some mornings, looking out of my bedroom window, I feel like I'm buried up to my eyes.

The sun rises behind the hill, which is to say behind the graveyard, so it rises later for me, and for my neighbors, than it does for the rest of the town. How can I but blame the dead for this, for the lateness of dawn, the diminution of light? But maybe the dead see it differently: my neighbors and I get an extra hour of peace before the light clambers through our windows and, like the noise of dog chains and car doors and garbage cans rolled up and down driveways, prods us awake.

Some mornings, when I look out of my bedroom window, the graveyard seems like another town: one that carries on all the same business as the one where I live, but is dead.

It's a reasonably well-tended cemetery, the grass is mowed every other week, and at least some of the graves—the stones whose inscriptions are large enough for me to read from my window—bear the marks of frequent patronage. Nor is it very crowded, affixed as it is to the church on the corner, the Episcopal church I can see if I lean close enough to my window. The church's membership has been in steady decline, and this being a members-only cemetery, very few new bodies are added each year. Behind the sacristy is a dumpster full of discarded pews. The enormous downed limb of a century-old oak lies beside it, like the arm of the rightful heir to the Castle of Otranto. A few of the taller monuments have been knocked over, or lifted off their pedestals, and one is broken in half across its middle. Vandalism? Possibly. I would rather call them signs of the broader declension of our town.

For those of us living across from the graveyard, the chief attractions are the relative quiet of having only half as many living neighbors, the somber aesthetic of the stones, and the music of the church bells, which resonate with particular beauty against the hillside, the stones acting like the sounding vases in an old amphitheater. It's said the priest still pulls the rope himself, though I don't see how this could be true. I sometimes see him puttering between the church and his little house across the driveway, its chimney smoking like a crematorium. His small congregation is similarly advanced in age; I don't think all of them together would weigh enough to ring the bells. But perhaps church bells have gone the way of compound bows in archery; one needn't be a Quasimodo to ring them anymore.

Suffice to say it's a dying church, a dying congregation—and a dying graveyard, if that isn't too much of an oxymoron. And what's true of the church is true of the town, though you wouldn't know it at a glance. To the unaccustomed eye, the flush of its cheeks—the bustle and hum of activity; the passing salutes to neighbors, as though pressing business begrudged even a handshake; the money changing hands and changing back again—all this might easily be mistaken for health. In truth, it's the sign of a lingering fever.

At the top of the hill, the top of the graveyard, is a still-wooded knoll, an island of trees, known for a place where the indigent sleep in the summer. This is where he came from, one morning when I was looking out of my bedroom window, an hour earlier than I usually rise, and just before dawn.

If you've never witnessed a man emerging from a cemetery before it has opened for the day, it would be difficult to explain exactly why it is so disquieting. I wondered whether I had ever created a similar impression in my neighbors, who might have noticed me wandering around the cemetery without having seen me enter through the mower's gate, and without recognizing me.

I didn't recognize him for a neighbor, either. But it would be more proper to say I didn't recognize him for a man. He appeared at first like a disembodied pair of legs: the operating-room remainders of a double amputee that had somehow managed to unbury themselves. Perhaps the torso, and the head, like the smaller inscriptions on the more distant stones, simply refused to resolve. Or perhaps some trick of the light had thrust his legs much closer to me than the rest of him; and, like a man stretched along the gradient of a strong gravitational field, he had distended to match the contour of the hillside. I understand this is the opposite of what should have happened: even with the sun still buried in the earth, the light should have caught his head first, and thrown *that* down the hill at me, like the horseman did at Sleepy Hollow. As if he were built upsidedown, head dragging along the earth; or as if he walked on all fours with his waist thrust up in the air, and his feet pointed toward me.

Once I understood that it was a man—once, that is, I was a little more awake, and something I recognized as the upper half of a body materialized atop the legs—I suspected him of being one of the indigents who slept on the knoll. I suspected he was a drunk, a drug addict, a vandal, who knew what sort of ghoul. Shrinking a little from my window, I waited for him to knock over a stone. After all, anyone who sleeps in a graveyard—anyone who would take the dead for his bedfellows—has compromised himself. But it's also true that I judged him less by the direction from which he came than by his odd manner of locomotion. He would stand for a moment the way swimmers used to take their marks, but pigeon-toed, and wilting slightly. Then he would collapse against the nearest stone. After taking several moments to right himself, swaying back and forth the whole time, he would stand just as he had before—and then collapse again, this time against the *next* nearest stone. In this way, using the stones for anchors, tossed from one to the next on a hillside that seemed to pitch and roll like a heavy sea, he made a zig-zagging course toward the fence.

In the meantime the sun had edged closer to rising, and the hilltop began to glow like the island of trees was on fire. I formulated a more charitable fantasy about him: that he was responsible for dragging the sun up over the hill. He moved, I thought now, like the sun was a too-heavy sack of potatoes he carried on his shoulder. I had risen early enough to witness something most mortals never did, the labor involved in getting the sun up over the horizon. At least my horizon: the stunted horizon of my little street, with its dying church on the corner and its graveyard on a hill. Gods, fairies, all sorts of wonders become visible if you just wake up early enough, or stay up late enough, past town-imposed curfews and now-I-lay-me-down-to-sleep.

The nearer he got to the fence that separated the graveyard from my street—the nearer the sun came to the rim of the hill—the less crooked his path became, and the fewer stones he required for support. Slowly, he released himself from their gravity, and pitched himself into his own wide orbit. At first he walked with his arms thrown out, like a man on a beam. But soon his arms came down toward his sides, his legs straightened, and his knees and toes pointed forward, though his feet shuffled like the grass was coated with ice, and he stooped noticeably. All this created yet another impression in me: that he was teaching himself to walk, guided by the dead who, like doting parents, passed him from one stone to another. I decided that he must do this every morning, in the time it took him to descend the hillside. As though it took years, instead of minutes, for him to traverse the distance between the knoll and the fence; as though I had been standing at my window for years, watching him, watching this day, come into being.

Perhaps it was the steadily-improving light, or his nearness to my window; but he *did* resolve, the way the inscriptions on some of the further headstones do in the late afternoon, when the sun has begun to fall behind my house. He wasn't the ghoul I had initially taken him for, his clothes weren't the rags I had expected. He was, in fact, perfectly presentable. A jacket, the arms cut a little short, but otherwise neatly trimmed to his thin frame; slacks that appeared to have been recently pressed, and without a trace of dirt on the knees; his shoes shone, though this might have been the dew collected on their toes. Atop his head—a head that had unfolded like the bud of a clean-shaven flower—was a wide-brimmed hat, the sort you might see in photographs of nineteenth-century rustics, or itinerant preachers. He was about my age, I guessed, perhaps a little older—yes, a little older, though just a hair—a year or two, five at most.

I watched him reach over the mower's gate and lift the latch. The movement was so clearly familiar to him that I realized it was *his* gate, as much as the one between my yard and driveway was mine. The hinges squeaked, again when he closed the gate behind him. And just as he crossed the threshold—somehow I predicted this, a moment before it happened—the sun broke like a tide over the trees on the knoll. That squeak, it was no longer the gate; it was the light, it was the sun rubbing like a balloon across the hide of the earth. I understood that it was the sound, not the light, that had always woken me, when I would look up from my pillow and see the light beginning its slow, bladelike descent of the wall above my head; the squeak was the sound of the blade overcoming its rusty inertia. Dazzled, I shielded my eyes just in time to catch sight of him, or his shadow, crossing in the direction of the sidewalk, of the houses—of my house—before he disappeared under the roof of my porch.

For a moment I was certain—I was terrified—that he was coming to *my* door; and I held my breath, listening for the proverbial loose board (one among many, I'm afraid), the rustle of the Indian corn hanging on the screen, the laying of his knuckles against my door. I had an appointment with him, I had simply forgotten, and after he had retrieved me, I would go back with him the way he had come, trailing slightly behind, until, by the time we had reached the knoll, we were headless, crawling, bony things feeling around for an open grave. By this time the sun would have gone down—it would have gone down the moment he entered the graveyard again, the light just fading from the inscriptions that all faced my way; somehow a whole day would have passed, a whole season, a whole life. I couldn't turn around, I was so sure I would see him standing in my doorway, bathed in light, looking even more dapper and assured than he had passing the gate, his hat held in his hands.

But there was no loose board, no knock, no moldering whiff in my nostrils announcing his presence, and no thin well-dressed man framed in my bedroom doorway, a little pale from walking always with his back to the sun. I turned to my window again in time to see him emerge from under the roof of the porch, heading in the direction of the church, the direction of town. His feet no longer shuffled, not even a little, no, he walked with the exaggerated high-stepping gait of a parade marshal. Chin up, stoop gone, steaming like a well-cover, all God's light upon him: he was a man now, indeed a man, ready to take his place among the men of the town, ready to make his mark.

As I pressed my face against the glass to watch him, a cloud passed over me: I was sure I was witnessing the arrival of a plague. I had the absurd idea of running to the church to pull the bell-rope, to alert the town of his coming. But I stayed there at my window, watching, until the sun had climbed clear of the ridge, and he had disappeared around the corner. I might have followed him, out of curiosity, if nothing else. Except that I was sure I would no longer recognize him—that, by the time he reached the center of town, he would look just like everyone else, lost in the crowd and the bustle of the morning.

THE DISTURBED THINGS

HE AWOKE AND, GAZING AROUND THE ROOM IN THE MORNING LIGHT, noticed things had moved. The chair was angled a little more toward the window. The desk was pulled slightly away from the wall, as if to retrieve a pencil fallen behind it. The picture, of a ship cocked and foundering in heavy swells, a little crooked the previous evening, hung straight. The bottom drawer of the dresser was open a hair.

Rising, he carefully restored the things to their original places.

The next morning, they were disturbed again, though not in exactly the same way.

Perhaps because nothing went missing, he thought little of it. He could have simply misremembered where things were. But eventually the feeling caught up with him: he wondered *why* he thought so little of it. Because they were not *his* things? He hardly used the chair, with its moldy cushions and worn-out springs. Or the desk, except to pile his few books. He didn't even look at the picture very often.

His things—the books, change of clothes, coat, shoes (two pairs) and overshoes, framed photo of himself as a boy, marbled pebbles, sea-shell bits, Navy figurine (admiral), tea cups (two), wooden trunk with frayed handles—did not move, except insofar as they found themselves upon things that did.

It would have been one thing had the things been disturbed in the daytime. The charwoman had a key. He tried to be in when she cleaned, irregular though she was. He would help her slide the trunk, and the iron frame of the bed; the charwoman, unlike the landlady, was petite. She would tease him about not trusting her with his things, saying, *Do you think I don't have a man to buy me all the things I want? You silly goose.* But if the day was sufficiently overcast he would go to the park, to feed the pigeons the breadcrusts he had gathered off the other boarders' plates before the cook could turn them into pudding; or to the library (but never to read).

The charwoman was much too diligent for the dust to accumulate to a degree that the disturbed things would leave a trace. He might pay her *not* to clean. But he was afraid of calling attention to himself. Instead, he bought a yardstick. Each morning, before going down to breakfast, he took measurements: from the top corners of the picture to the ceiling; from the front leg of the chair to a pencil mark on the baseboard, along a line parallel to the adjacent wall; and so on. Logging each day's figures, perusing them while pigeons gamboled over him or vagrants snored in nearby chairs, he was able to verify that the disturbances were real—though so subtle, and so irregular (no direction; no determinable pattern, though he subjected the figures to endless mental algorithms) that he was unable to entirely remove the suspicion that his measurements had been taken in such a way as to validate his impressions.

What if the charwoman, or the landlady, or another boarder who had somehow gotten hold of his key, was creeping into his room to disturb things while he slept? Sitting down to breakfast one morning, in one of the slatted chairs that made his hips ache—there was not a comfortable chair in the whole place, he said to himself, though never aloud—while the cook was rattling the cutlery in the kitchen, he inquired, as discreetly as he could, of his fellow boarders. *It's funny*, he began—and for one who was hardly known to speak at all, there was something momentous in so inauspicious a beginning—*it's funny, but some days I forget where things are. Stuff is just … out of place.* Not quite where I thought it was. And then he scanned the other faces at the table for a meaningful look, a signal to arrange a clandestine meeting. Circumambulating the pond in the hollow at the park's center, the one with the toy sailboats, a secret would be divulged: about another boarder, or the charwoman (she occasionally smelled), or the landlady, or the landlady's deceased husband, whose picture sat on the mantle beneath his ludicrously small rapier.

No one took his bait. Not Ong, mostly blind, who continued to squint at him expectantly through his thick glasses. Not Fitzgerald, who seemed to nourish himself entirely on his own fingernails. Not Czerny, "the Pole," a philosopher, retired from the University of Sczrenzk (or so it was rumored), who spent all day on the bench in the corner of the foyer, where the light was poorest, reading; he even had a book open beside his plate. And not any of the salesmen stopping through, with their suitcases full of Bibles or brassieres or whatnot, whose names he never quite learned, or as quickly forgot, one of whom (that particular morning) had the most perfect teeth. Like him, they did not want to call attention to themselves. And so no one spoke at all, until one of the salesmen (the other one) began his pitch for the boarders, opening his briefcase on the table. The Pole did not even look up.

Had he considered the possibility that the boarding-house was haunted? The lodgings were suspiciously cheap. The house was two centuries old. The history of the neighborhood was sanguinary (a suppressed meatpackers' strike; potter's field by the river). Perhaps he was sensitive to such things, and had never been in a situation to know. At first he thought it must be the spirit of some boarder who had died in the room; but eventually he settled on the deceased husband of the landlady as the most likely candidate. For a military man, he was quite frail-looking, at least at the time the picture had been taken. The landlady said so little about him, and her answers to the salesmen's periodic questions were so equivocal, that one was left to invent what was likely a much more colorful character than had actually lived, and certainly than appeared in the picture. His death was a source of endless speculation—though all agreed that foul play was involved, and that the landlady was responsible (inheritance, mistress, spite). Regardless, he never got the sense, from the subtle movements of the furniture, that a spirit was trying to communicate anything. Nor did he feel in any way threatened, as though the widowers and retirees who now occupied the house were suitors encroaching on the deceased husband's one-time property. It hardly squared with the picture, or with the nutcracker-sized weapon hanging over the mantle. He himself had never imagined the landlady in this way. The charwoman was more his type. She would bend over to help him move his trunk; she would get down on her hands and knees to fish things out from behind the desk.

In the end, he could only conclude that the spirit spent its nights going in and out of rooms like his, looking for things that belonged to it. Perhaps, by moving things, it was simply acting on the memory of how they had used to be arranged. In fact, his very room might have belonged—might *belong* to the spirit; the room was no more his than the furniture. And he might have grown comfortable with this, except that the spirit, whose sympathy and companionship he sought, could never make up its mind from one night to the next. Over time, this indecision began to weigh on him. He grew impatient, and then contemptuous, leaping out of bed to slide the chair (for example) further than the spirit could have moved it in a month, and then sneering at it from his pillow.

Until the night came that he announced to the room that he did not believe in ghosts.

The very next morning, the things were more disturbed than ever. Which is to say, hardly at all.

He began a series of experiments to try to discover the motive force behind the disturbed things. He still had not discarded the possibility of an intruding boarder, perhaps in cahoots with the thuggish landlady, or the lascivious charwoman, whom he imagined watching him sleep from the sagging chair with a calf on either armrest. First he had to rule *himself* out—the possibility, that is, that he was the spirit in question: the one rising in the middle of the night to disturb the things. Him, or some heretofore hidden part of him, buried so deep that it did not even surface in his dreams. It was for this reason he had never measured the bed: if he jerked or tossed, the bed might shift slightly—unlikely, given its mass, but not impossible—and then the only thing he would be measuring was the force of his own (involuntary) night-movements. But this was precisely what he set out to capture now. He filled his bedpan with cold water from the bathroom at the end of the hall, and, on successive nights, set it before the chair, the desk, the dresser, and the picture. On each following morning, he awoke to find the floor dry, the bedpan still full—and the things disturbed. He tried again, this time stringing wire around the room through eyehooks he screwed into the baseboard, in a crisscrossing spiderweb he unwove on each of three consecutive mornings. And then again with carpet tacks, distributed in a checkerboard pattern around the floor, and with identical results—which is to say, none—the only difference being that, in the morning, he managed to step on a tack.

He began sitting up after the lamp was out to peer around the room, his eyes slowly adjusting to the dark, listening, motionless, silent. To see the chair or the picture spin, the desk slide; to hear the groan of old legs against the floorboards, the cry of inertia violated … The close attention soon exhausted him, and he nodded off to the too-familiar sounds of the other boarders going about their nightly business (Fitzgerald playing the piano in the parlor two floors below, sometimes accompanying the landlady; Ong's tinny radio; the salesmen practicing their pitches, like preachers in their closets; the radiators; the bathroom pipes, running, always running; inebriates' laughter; mattress springs), as well as some less-familiar noises, perhaps half-dreamed, and magnified by his awareness, until they almost seemed to be in the room with him. Some nights, he blew out the lamp and then re-lit it right away, murmuring an excuse to himself, as though to trick an invisible presence. But the changes never came so quickly. The things might have taken the whole night to accomplish their modest peregrinations; if so, they would have gone about their business slowly indeed—more slowly than he could hope to observe. Like the hour hand of a clock, process was a cipher; he could only tell difference, or believe he could tell the difference, between what *was* and what *had been*.

And yet, there were nights when he would rise and, groping his way around, become absolutely certain that things were in wildly different places than they had been when he had gone to sleep. Lighting the lamp (if he could find it; for how could he be certain the lamp would still be on the dresser, the dresser by the bed?), he would find everything just as it had been—or that things had suddenly returned to their places with the influx of light, like naughty children pretending to be asleep. As though the light itself had stitched the room back together. But then how to account for the difference, mornings, when the light, forgetful, did not always put things back just the way they had been? Was it the senility of the light he was witnessing? Perhaps the room in darkness was simply not the same room as the room in light. Each night, he passed over a gulf that could not be bridged; and each day, despite the apparent persistence of things, was entirely discontinuous from the one before.

It came to him at last: the room. There was no other possible remaining explanation. He would take advantage of the next vacancy to request a move. When it came, the landlady was immediately suspicious. Was there a problem with *his* room? Oh, no, it was fine, he assured her. He just wanted a change. She said nothing for a time, though from the way she looked at him he began to wish he had invented a problem, or at least a preference: the view, say—this though the newly-vacated room was on the floor below, and he was not much for looking out of windows anyway. The landlady rose and began to attend to random business around her office. It was as if she were awaiting a confession. And he was just beginning to wonder if the interview was over when she lifted the keyring big as a jailer's from the nail under the mailboxes and said, without looking at him, *Well, come along, then.* Rather than leading him to the vacancy, she took him back to his own room, which she opened with her own key; and she proceeded to carry out an inspection more meticulous than ever the charwoman had, while he stood nakedly at the door. With her there, lifting up the corner of the mattress, opening the dresser drawers, peering under the furniture and the window curtain, even nudging the trunk with her foot—with her there, *everything* seemed out of place. The inspection, which might have lasted five minutes, seemed to take much longer; the charwoman even poked her head in at one point, and he had to suffer hearing his request relayed to her in the most ridiculous and unfavorable terms. If she noticed either the eyeholes or the pencil marks, she gave no indication. In the end, she withdrew without a word, and he followed her back to her office, where she handed him a new key, reminding him to return the old one as soon as he was finished transferring his things.

An indescribable sadness came over him when he beheld his new lodgings. The chair was the same—mold-blossom on the cushions, exhausted springs—just upholstered in a different pattern. The desk was identical. Even the picture had a maritime theme, one similarly ominous. As for the view: it was true he could no longer look out (as he seldom did) over the tarred beaches, with their broken chimneys and steaming vents and hanging wash. The sawtooth roofs of the row-houses across the street did present a physically different scene. But it was identical, he thought, in character. And here the landlady had led him to believe that the rooms for transients were somehow more attractive than those for so-called residents, and as such that she was potentially sacrificing business to a whim of his. Drawing the curtain and sitting down on the edge of the bed, he could only wonder if she hadn't been right.

It took him less time to carry down most of his things than it had taken the landlady to perform her inspection. His books made up the first load; the second, a single dresser drawer's worth of clothes, shoes, and overshoes (the other was empty); then his toilet items and knick-knacks, arranged in the desk drawer (the picture of himself as a boy, dwarfed by its pewter frame; the admiral, tall as a salt-shaker, the paint chipping from his cap; pebbles and sea shells and tea cups). That left only the trunk. It was heavier than he remembered. He went for the Pole. His reasons were several: he knew exactly where to find him; he distrusted him less than anyone else in the house; and (this related to the second reason) he sensed a total indifference to anything outside the world of his books. About the last, however, he proved to be mistaken. "Vhat inside?" the Pole asked, after they had slid the trunk under the nearly-identical bed of the nearly-identical room. He confessed he did not know, or perhaps did not remember. (It amounted to the same thing.) He could not know, he explained, because the trunk was locked, and he did not have the key. In fact, he could not even remember how he had acquired the trunk in the first place. The Pole seemed incredulous, or perhaps only confused; it was possible he had not understood. Then he asked, sensibly enough, "Vhere is key?" Again, he confessed not to know. The Pole pondered this for a time, gnawing on his white mustache with his lower teeth, as he often did over his books. He seemed on the point of saying something. Then he shrugged and, measuring the room with one quick glance, departed.

Before returning the key, he went back and took a last look at his old room, at the old things that seemed newly lifeless, before locking the door.

The new bed received him just as the old one had: with the embrace of a corpse.

The next morning, he awoke to find the new things disturbed: chair pulled out a little from the wall, desk at an angle, picture crooked (the ship was almost vertical now; the sea, crooked), top dresser drawer open a hair. At first he blamed the unfamiliarity of the space— or rather, its strange mixture of familiarity and unfamiliarity. Disoriented, he had simply tried to map the arrangement of the new things onto the old—a natural enough response to his long tenancy in the other room. It was nothing of the sort. Rather, it was as though the old things had followed him here, clamoring, *And us?* Or as though he had only imagined he had moved. He was afraid to look out the window and see the tarred beaches again.

At breakfast he scanned the faces of his fellow boarders with a silent intensity that had been absent from the innocent query of a few weeks before. He watched the cook, and the charwoman as she bustled through, and the landlady when she entered to bid her boarders good-morning, as she occasionally did—and then to ask *him*, oh! most insidiously, *how he found his new lodgings!* His eyes dropped to his plate; he felt all the other eyes at the table upon him. She left before he could think how to answer. Then the prattle of the salesmen began again, and the clink of silverware, and he slowly resumed eating.

He spent the remainder of the morning sitting on his trunk, staring at his big toe through a hole in his sock. Not the room, then: the things themselves. The things themselves were disturbed. Not an action; a condition. This did not bother him. What bothered him was that they would target *him* in this way. Could they sense he did not love them? He had never abused them—carved his initials into a desk, say, or spilled hot tea on the upholstery, or worn the springs of the saddled mattresses yet further. But he supposed he had neglected them. The god of things had grown offended by his lack of attention. And yet, *they were not his things.* He felt the need to stress this again, hoping the god was listening. They did not share his past; they were as alien to him as the other boarders. It was not *his* fault that the chair was broken, the desk useless, the picture depressing, the mattress saddled. In fact, *he* was the one who had to deal with the ache in his hips and back, who had to stare at that image of imminent maritime doom every day. If anyone had the right to be aggrieved, it was him.

"If you have a problem," he said to the chair, "I suggest you take it up with the landlady. You are not my responsibility."

The chair did not reply, just sat there at its harumphing angle to the wall, conspiring, in its silent way, with the rest of the furniture about where to go next.

And yet, he was on the most intimate terms with them. They were the last things he saw before he blew out the lamp each night, the first things to greet him when he opened his eyes each morning. He might spurn them, curse them inwardly, but that did not alter the fact of their marriage. The thought troubled him. For *his* few things—the things he liked to think of as his; the things he had carried from one room to another—had never participated in these nightly revolutions, except unwittingly. What little he did have was nothing if not well-loved (he wriggled his toe at this thought). Or would the true lover of things have mended the sock? Perhaps the time was coming when they would join the mutiny, like conflicted crewmembers who at last decide to risk the yardarm.

It was too strong a word, mutiny. It was not as though, waking, he found these unloved things encroaching upon him, like malevolent figures in wax. He did not have nightmares about the chair swinging down and cracking open his skull, or the bed overturning like a swamped dory. But he did, in the coming days, begin to dream their movements more grand and ludic: cloistering together at the center of the room, or amassing in a single corner, the desk pushed up behind the chair, the latter's legs in the air, revealing, perhaps, engraved initials (his?), or a wad of dried chewing gum (his?); the picture hanging sideways, or upside-down, the troubled ocean a sky, the ailing ship a crooked chandelier—and, in the grub-white rectangle where it had hung, a hole, with a rolled-up letter stuffed inside (his?), or a tooth swaddled in fabric (his?)—or nothing, except a tunnel-view into another's room (his?), someone he did not know, or did not recognize—someone, anyway, who did not belong there. In his dreams even his own things joined the melee, if more sheepishly than the rest: his shoes chose a partner from the other pair, and of the same foot; his slacks, which he habitually hung with the cuffs toward him, turned so that he could see the waist instead; his pebbles and shells arranged themselves into scant constellations; the admiral commandeered one or another of the tea cups. But the dreams faded as soon as he opened his eyes, and saw the things again in their slightly-out-of-place places. It was a mutiny of sorts: this is what the dreams were trying to tell him. They whittled dully at him, bored holes in him so small he did not bleed, peeled away the rind that was, finally, all of him.

He gathered his own things to him before they could go the way of his dreams: his change of clothes, which he wore along with his coat, and a hostage shoe from either pair, together with his overshoes. He filled his pockets with the pebbles and shells, admiring their ballast; the admiral he held before him like a crucifix. And he watched, from his trunk, the desk and chair and dresser and bed—the bed!—as they floated a hair's-breadth above the floor. Unmoored, yes. But it was more than that. They had become weirdly … fungible. He could not think of a better word. They were not altogether there.

They said the same about him: the other boarders; the charwoman; the salesmen; the landlady, eventually. He had not been to the park or library in weeks, despite the pleasant overcast of days. He had stopped coming down to breakfast. They said he had lost weight, that he looked pale, unkempt. The cook even prepared a draught for him. He told them he was not sleeping well. It was true. How could he sleep, curled up on a trunk half as long as he was and hardly wider than his shoulders, on uneven wood slats, nail-heads, and metal braces?

The charwoman brought him soup and crustless bread to sop it with. He slurped quietly, hardly daring to steal a glance at her. He understood he might be evicted for illness; to have a boarder die here would cast a pall over the whole establishment. It was a terrible place to think of haunting. Frowning at his pallor, the charwoman told him he looked a mite better. She took the half-empty bowl with her, while he settled in to await the landlady's heavy knock, her knuckles like brass couplings. She would come, he was sure, with the evidence of breadcrusts stolen, a murdered pigeon, a befouled yardstick and drowned book of figures, and a toy sailboat with its pencil-thin mast snapped off, a mouse's nest on its deck.

He awoke and, gazing around the room in the morning light, realized things were just where they were supposed to be: the desk pushed up firmly against the wall, the chair at its proper angle, the drawers of the dresser firmly shut, the picture nearly straight.

And so was he: in bed, although he could not recollect moving. He sat up weakly, stared at his stocking feet—he could not recollect removing his shoes, either. None of his toes were visible, since none of the holes between the two pairs of socks he wore were aligned. Holding to the nearest bedpost, he slowly pulled himself erect, the mattress-springs groaning with him. He felt, he thought, what an animal must feel emerging from hibernation.

He removed the coat, and then the rest of the change of clothes, smoothing them as best he could, folding the slacks over his chair, waist toward him, and the shirt and socks into his dresser drawer, which he did not close entirely.

There: he could see the toe again. It did not wriggle.

From the coat pockets he took the picture and the cups, and then the admiral, lay them across his desk one piece at a time, and then emptied the pebbles and shells by the handful onto the trunk. The sound they made was unfamiliar. He leaned close, knocked on the lid; the pebbles and shells jumped. He pulled up on one frayed handle; the pebbles and shells skittered to the other end. Even in his wasted condition he was able to lift the trunk easily. He would not need the Pole to help him carry it now.

Someone had removed the mirror from the bathroom. It wasn't the first time; it was small enough to conceal. The salesmen, he thought. He splashed the face he could not see, expectorated into the sink. Then he went down to breakfast.

They all noticed him, of course. Even the Pole looked up. He looked at each of them in turn; he would make sure to look the land-lady in the eye, too, if she poked her head in to sing good-morning. He would stare boldly at the charwoman's bosom and legs as she flit-ted through, though she would pretend not to notice. And as he went to take his customary place at the table, he paused, and then—moved his chair ever so slightly to the left. Or was it to the right? It hardly mattered. He looked up to see if anyone had noticed. Surely they would notice once he was sitting? The daring new angle at which his chair stood to the table, at which he stood to them? He was the admi-ral in his teacup, braving the swells.

The problem was that no one looked directly at him. Oh, they spoke to him, they addressed their words to him, wished him well, told him they were glad to see he was feeling better, that he was look-ing like his old self again. They even toasted his health with their tea or juice. But whenever they looked in his direction, he got the sense they were looking somewhere else: at some entity standing directly behind him, say, and ever so slightly to one side.

When the cook put the soft-boiled egg in front of him, it was shifted to one side, as if for some other boarder; as if, should he at-tempt to eat it, his knife would slide down the shell, again and again, like a pigeon skittering off a cupola.

He dropped his knife, threw his napkin down, and rose so quick-ly his knees banged the underside of the table. The others clearly no-ticed, because they all looked at one another, and then interrupted their own breakfasts as well. Even the salesmen came along; and when the charwoman appeared, they silently but emphatically motioned for her to join them. As a group they pursued him into the foyer, first watching as he tottered up to the landing to wrestle with the grandfather clock, grunting; and then as he tottered back down to the foyer, to the bench where the Pole would sit to read, and the sewing chest with its vase of dying flowers. They stood in the door of the parlor, watching him rearrange furniture—or at least seeming to; for each time he stepped away from something—the settee, the piano and bench, the coffee table, the tassel-shaded lamp—and despite his obvious efforts, they could not detect any difference. He paused before the picture of the landlady's deceased husband, holding to the edges of the frame. But when he had stepped away, it was no less crooked.

By the time the landlady arrived, calling his name from the parlor door, he had taken her dead husband's rapier down from the mantle and was leaping back and forth with it, thrusting and parrying with an invisible enemy; and all the other boarders had begun to applaud.

ACKNOWLEDGMENTS

The stories in this collection were originally published, in slightly different form, as follows: "Fat Kid" in *Memorious* 23 (Dec. 2014); "The Death of the Pianist" in *Booth*, 30 Jan. 2015 (and subsequently in *Booth* 8); "Scarecrow" in *Washington Square* (Winter/Spring 2015) (under title "Sehnsucht"); "Burning Child" in *Washington Square* (Summer/Fall 2013); "The Hotel Fire" in *Cimarron Review* 189 (Fall 2014); "Ambergris" in *The Gettysburg Review* 30.4 (Winter 2017); "The Stability of Floating Bodies" in *New Ohio Review* 19 (Spring 2016); "The Technologies of Pucks" in *Conjunctions* online, 29 Oct. 2019; "The Pond" in Zone 3 29.2 (Fall 2013); "Carls" in *New Ohio Review* 35 (Winter 2025); "Graveyard" in *Juked*, 30 June 2019; "The Disturbed Things" in *PANK*, 1 Nov. 2020.

Thanks to the patient editors at many of these journals who helped make these stories better. Thanks also to the photographer at the Goatwhore/Three Inches of Blood show at St. Vitus who took the picture of fat kid. Thanks to the technicians at Gramercy Typewriters and the now-defunct Typewriters & Things for keeping my Remington Quiet-Riters 10 and 11 loudly humming, and me with them. Thanks to my union, the Professional Staff Congress, for the grant to help me kickstart this collection. And thanks to everyone at New American Press for believing in this bloody little book.

"The Disturbed Things" was inspired by the Roman Polanski film *The Tenant*, as well as by Hawthorne. The phrase "insidious latent life" appears in Roger Greaves's translation of *The Haunted Screen*, to which the epigraph of "The Hotel Fire" belongs.

CRAIG BERNARDINI'S stories and essays have appeared in *AGNI, Conjunctions* online, *The Gettysburg Review, New Ohio Review*, and many other lovely journals. A graduate of Johns Hopkins (B.A., The Writing Seminars) and the University of Utah (Ph.D., English), he is a Professor of English at Hostos Community College, a City University of New York School in the Bronx. He lives in the mid-Hudson Valley with his partner, dogs, and chickens (cats RIP).

www.ingramcontent.com/pod-product-compliance
Lightning Source LLC
Chambersburg PA
CBHW030825020726
47499CB00006B/2068